WHEN MONSTERS FIGHT

THE MONSTERS AMONG US BOOK 5

DEBBIE CASSIDY

CONTENTS

CHAPTER 1

RUE

The last thing I expected when I fell asleep was to dream walk into Gehenna and meet a battle-worn woman claiming to be Lucifer. Lucifer, as in the devil from our old human texts. Lucifer, who was meant to be evil personified, but this woman, although brash and cranky, didn't exude evilness. And if she was real, if this place was real, then it meant... "Is this Hell?"

She made a sound of exasperation as if my question was an irritant. "Hell is one of its many names, and it's hardly important now. I must determine what has happened. If God didn't send you, then how can you be here?"

God? She thought *God* sent me, which meant she didn't know. "God is long gone."

Her eyes flew wide for a moment before narrowing and taking her mouth into a thin line. "Of course he is, but if you're here, then you are a part of the plan, whether you realize it or not." She lifted her chin, looking down her nose at me. "Tell me everything you know. Now."

My pulse raced, my gut telling me that she was the piece of the puzzle we were missing, and if I could lay everything I knew on the table, she'd help me make sense of it.

But where to start? Deep breath. "Over twenty years ago, the Morningstar fractured." I filled her in on the fall of the celestials, the monsters coming out of Gehenna, the watchers, the Golden City, our search for the relic pieces, and finally on Shem...my Shem, and his valiant sacrifice. "If I can find the final piece, then I can put everything to rights." I looked about the room. "Something brought me here. To you. Which means you're important in this. Can you help me? I need to finish what Shem started."

"This Shem...he fractured the relic?"

"Yes, but he was under the influence of—"

"Yes...yes, I understand." Her gaze flit from side to side. "But you say that Michael ended him?"

A lump formed in my throat. "Yes."

She muttered something under her breath that I didn't catch before nodding as if to herself. "I told him not to trust the Dominion. I warned him. He was always too benevolent for his own good. He should have kept me by his side. Allowed me to protect him. He would never have simply left. No. We had a plan, and he would have honored his word to me." She seemed to drift off into her own thoughts.

"What plan?"

She blinked sharply. "There's no time for that now. If you want to stop the Dominion, you must bring me the relic pieces you have."

"What? Why?"

She smiled humorlessly. "*He* had a nickname for me, inspired by the intensity of my unique power. The way it shone...He called me his Morningstar."

My breath caught. "What are you saying?"

"You know what I'm saying, child. The Morningstar belongs to me. It's a part of my soul kept safe by him. He used it to maintain the balance between the worlds he created. A way for him to keep a piece of me close." A wry smile painted her lips for a moment. "But it's time for me to reclaim it and become whole."

God used part of her soul to create the relic? "I don't have all the pieces, and even if I did, I'm not sure I should bring them to you. If the relic maintains the boundaries between our worlds, then what will happen if you absorb it?"

"The balance will be restored. I can promise you that much. You will have your world back, and the celestials will be forced to come back to heaven."

There was no deception in her tone. "You can do that?"

"Once restored I can. I swear it to you. It is not possible for me to speak an untruth."

Like the watchers...They hated lies. Did that come from her? From the Morningstar because it was built from her power? It must be.

I believed her words. I believed her with every fiber of my being. "Okay. But I need to find the final piece first."

Cold fire bloomed in her eyes. "A star fell over two decades ago. I felt its impact and longed to go to it. But I'm limited on how far I can travel through Gehenna. This world is made up of nine planes, and I can only move through four of them. The star is in the fifth."

"You think this star is a piece of the relic?"

"I didn't think of it at the time, but now, after all you've revealed, I believe that it must be. Now that I know what's happened, the strange behavior of the creatures in the inner three planes makes sense. This world is fragmenting, seeping out through the fractures caused by the Morningstar's destruction."

She crossed the room and stopped a foot away from me. This close, she not only towered over me, but seemed... larger, as if she'd been compacted into this skin—raw power begging to be released. Power that now licked at my skin.

"The chosen watcher has fallen," she said, her tone thrumming with a reverence that made my chest ache. "It is now up to you to complete his quest. You must find the entrance to Gehenna, travel to this central plane, and set me free. It's the only way to save not only your world, but many more."

Her visage rippled, and the room around me began to fade. "Something's happening. I think I'm waking up."

She gripped my shoulders, the contact sending a shiver of power through me. "The fact that you are here means you are close to a convergence of power. Find it, and you will find a way to me."

"Convergence of power? What does that mean?"

Her grip on me faded, and so did the room around me, but hopeful, bright eyes remained fixed on me.

"Find me..."

I woke gasping for air, my heart pounding in my throat so hard I thought it might choke me.

"Rue! Rue, you're okay. It was just a nightmare," Bastian said.

He put his arm around me, coaxing me to lean against his chest. The contact grounded me, and my errant pulse calmed.

"I'll get some water," Bee said, scrambling to her feet across the dimly lit room.

I shook my head and held up my hand to stall her. "No... Wait...I'm fine. Not a nightmare. A revelation."

"What?" Sarq looked confused.

The yawning chasm of darkness that Shem's death had left inside me housed a pinprick of light because now we had real hope. "I know where the final piece of the relic is."

"What?" Bastian asked. "Where?"

"In Gehenna. Guys, we're going to Hell."

CHAPTER 2

If the church housed a doorway to Gehenna but also sat on an overlap of powerlines, which the watchers called a crossing, it would explain why this place was so special. Why it warded off monsters and hid from celestial eyes.

We were so close to finishing this. So close to fixing our world. "Okay, so we find this doorway, but first we need to locate the relic pieces Shem said he hid here."

"They're in the basement," Sarq said. "We have them hidden behind protective runes. I can get them once we know where we're taking them."

Good idea. Best to keep them hidden until we needed them.

"We'll have to tell Jilyana," Bee said. "She's housing a relic fragment inside her, remember, and she'll need to go to Gehenna too."

"But we *only* tell her that the fourth relic is in Gehenna," Gabriel said quickly. "The fact that Rue can piece it together or that we're taking the fragments to Lucifer must be kept secret until we have the final piece and it's time to head to Lucifer."

Bee frowned at me. "You don't trust her?"

"I want to trust her, Bee, but I need time to be sure. Best to err on the side of caution and only tell her everything when we have to."

Bee nodded. "Okay. We keep that piece of information between us. But then, how do we convince her that she needs to come with us?"

"I doubt she'll need convincing," Sarq said. "If it's a choice between remaining here with the other watchers or being with Rue..."

He had a good point. "We begin the search for a doorway into Gehenna tomorrow. The place isn't huge, and it shouldn't take too long to find it."

"Don't be so sure," Penemue said. "It could be a mere fracture right now. The fact that the other relic pieces are here could be what allowed you to connect to it and to Lucifer. We'll have to comb the grounds, and we can use Jilyana as a dousing rod. She houses a relic shard, and it'll be drawn to the convergence."

"That's a solid plan," Sarq said.

"There is something else we must consider, "Gabriel said. "Fractures work both ways."

It took me a moment to grasp what he was insinuating, and then my stomach dropped. "Our people aren't safe here."

If there was a fracture leading to Gehenna, then monsters could come through it.

"Nothing has come through yet," Sarq says. "This place repels monsters, remember?"

It did that right now, but... "What if that changes if we go through this convergence? What if us accessing the doorway changes the wards on this place or drops them completely? Our people would be in danger."

"Then we move them," Gabriel said.

"Move them? To where?"

"There *is* nowhere else," Tumiel said. "This is our last truly safe zone."

"It may be *your* last," Gabriel said. "But it isn't mine."

"What do you mean?"

"I mean I know of a safe place. A place filled with humans. The last stand. The resistance."

"RESISTANCE?" Sarq stared at Gabriel in confusion. "As in...a human resistance?"

"Yes," Gabriel said. "A human resistance."

"No, that can't be," Tumiel said. "We would have found them by now."

Gabriel gave him a wry smile. "Not without their precise location and access codes to their settlement."

"They have a settlement?" Bee asked, her eyes wide.

Gabriel nodded. "Rue, I told you I had information about the Dominion's plan on this." He held up the small metal object. "It's called a—"

"Flash drive," Bastian said. "But we'd need a computer to read it."

"And you'll have one at base zero."

"There is no base zero," Sarq said, but he didn't sound so sure.

"Not that the Dominion are aware of, no," Gabriel replied. "I made sure to keep it a secret when I organized the base setup decades ago."

"*You* were responsible for that?" Tumiel asked.

"Yes. I oversaw it all. Even back then, I suspected what the Dominion were planning. I understood that to have a chance at survival, humanity would need to be protected, not only from the monsters, but from the celestials themselves. I created a sector zero and provided the humans who lived there with the technology to maintain contact with me and the specific instructions to remain hidden. Over the past two decades, I've checked in with them regularly using longwave radio, but the past month, the Dominion security has been higher than usual, and so I've shut down communication to them. They were warned that I might have to do that, and if I don't contact them for more than eight weeks, then they should assume that I've been compromised and move their base."

"There are more humans out there?" Mira looked stunned.

"Yes. Yes, there are."

Puzzle pieces clicked into place. "The escape route out of the Golden City and the weapons...Those were for this resistance, weren't they?"

"Yes," Gabriel said.

Gabriel was a fucking genius.

"But we won't need any of that if we can get the relics to Lucifer," Erelim said.

"We still need to know what the Dominion are planning, though," Bastian added. "Right now, all you have is speculation. We need to see what's on that drive."

"And you'll find out." Gabriel held the drive out to Bastian.

Bastian frowned. "No...I...I need to stay with Rue."

"You can't," Gabriel said. "You're human, and Gehenna's atmosphere will kill you."

"Then why doesn't our atmosphere kill the monsters?" Bastian asked.

"Valid question," Bee said.

Gabriel sighed. "From what we've learned about the monsters and their biology, they're designed to adapt to their environment. However, when the reapers and I intercepted you on the road to the farmhouse, we detected sulfur in the air. Traces of an otherworld atmosphere. Their atmosphere."

The black mist. "Their world is seeping into ours, isn't it? Their atmosphere is tainting ours."

"Yes," Gabriel confirmed. "And if left unchecked, it will poison the air here." Bastian still hadn't taken the drive. "Please," Gabriel said. "I need you to get this to the resistance."

Bastian looked over at me, his expression torn because this meant splitting up. This meant two separate paths. It meant not knowing if the other was alive and well.

But Shem had died for this chance.

There was no other choice.

I swallowed the lump in my throat. "I'll focus better on getting the relics to Lucifer if I know our people have you watching their backs."

Bastian's shoulders slumped, but he took the drive, his jaw hard in that way that told me he was suppressing emotions. He fixed his gaze on Gabriel. "You'll keep Rue alive." It was a demand, not a question, and Gabriel took it as such, dropping Bastian a firm nod.

"You'll take Baraqel and his scouts with you," Sarq said. "We'll go with Rue."

But if my people were going to travel across monster-infested territory on foot, they needed all the protection they could get. "No, Sarq. I need you all to go with Bastian. The people need you."

"*You* need us," Sarq said. "Shem would want us to protect you."

"She'll be protected," Gabriel said. "I'm going with her."

"And she'll have me and my reapers," Erelim added. "We'll clear a path through the monsters in Gehenna."

"You'll attract the monsters with your light," Sarq pointed out. "You'll put them in danger."

"He's right, Erelim," Gabriel said. "Using the scythes here is beneficial, but if you use them in Gehenna, in a world created for monsters, then it's asking for trouble."

"You and Rue can't go alone," Erelim said. "It's much too dangerous."

He was right. But the reapers and the watchers weren't my only option of companion. "We won't be going alone. We'll have backup. We'll have Kabiel and the devolved to protect us."

"They can't get into the church," Zaq pointed out. "How will they get to the convergence?"

I had a plan for this too. "With enough celestial light to push them over the brink from monster to watcher."

Bastian sucked in a breath. "You're going to open the channel again?"

"Yes, and Jilyana will help me."

"The effects won't last long," Sarq said. "The changes never do."

"I know. They only need to last long enough to get the devolved through the convergence." I chewed on my cheeks, my mind whirring. "And Baraqel needs to be told the full truth. He can't be expected to protect the humans and keep fighting outside these walls without knowing exactly what he and his scouts are fighting for. Tell him to hold off on telling his scouts until I've left for Gehenna with Jilyana. I'll tell Jilyana the truth once we're in Gehenna and I have the fourth relic, just to be on the safe side."

"Hard to betray you if you're in hell," Bee said.

"It looks like we have a plan," Gabriel said.

Now all we needed to do was find the doorway to Gehenna.

A doorway hidden somewhere in this church.

CHAPTER 3

I washed my face and used the herbal concoction that Mira had created to clean my teeth. A new sense of urgency permeated every fiber of my being. Purpose. Direction. Focus. Our goal was so close now that I could taste it and the dangers that stood between us, and it, seemed trivial.

The study had emptied out except for Bastian who was busy folding the blankets and setting them to one side. "Sarq and Gabriel went to speak to Baraqel about base zero and the journey ahead, and Erelim is briefing the reapers. Bee is helping Mira get the humans organized. I doubt they'll be happy to know they've got to leave this place and go back out there."

"This place might not be safe once we open the convergence. They've got to go."

"I know. Mira and Bee will explain it to them. But...we agreed that we won't force people to leave if they decide to stay. If they want to stay, then they'll be staying here without watcher or reaper protection. Either way, we leave at dawn tomorrow."

Choice...something that had been taken from us for too long. "I don't want to lose lives, but...people deserve the right to decide how they want to live."

Bastian bridged the distance between us and cupped my shoulders. "I wish I could stay with you."

I wanted nothing more than to have him with me, but he was safer here than in Gehenna. There was no doubt in my mind on that, and I needed him safe. Alive. "I'll be back before you know it, and I'll find you. I'll always find you."

Bastian nodded, but there was darkness in his eyes, and it made my chest tight. But I didn't want to ask him about it. I didn't want to probe, because I didn't want to hear the answers—words that would remind me of his fast-approaching fate. Remind me how little time we had together, and how this...this being apart would eat into that.

Shem was dead.

Bastian was dying.

I couldn't save them, but I could save our world by freeing Lucifer and maybe...maybe she'd help me find a way to keep Bastian.

I placed my palm on his cheek. "I'm going to speak to Jilyana. You should prepare everyone for the journey to base zero."

He gently gripped my wrist then turned his head to kiss my palm. "I love you, Rue."

It sounded like goodbye, and the fog of numbness that had shrouded my heart lifted because I didn't like his tone. Not one bit.

I pushed up on my toes and crushed my lips to his in a hard, brief kiss. "You get to that base, and you wait for me. No heroics, Bastian. Yes, the people need you to get them to safety, but promise me you won't die for someone else's stupidity. Promise me you'll be waiting for me when I get back." I squeezed his nape. "Promise me."

He leaned in and rested his forehead against mine. "I swear it."

It would have to be enough.

I FOUND Jilyana standing by the altar staring up at the stained-glass windows which were bathed in morning sunlight. The room was a kaleidoscope of color that spilled over worn dark wood floors and bathed the whitewashed walls.

There was a tranquility about this place that calmed the turmoil in my chest for a beat, but then she looked my way with red-rimmed puffy eyes, and her pain echoed inside me.

"I can't believe that he's gone," she said softly. "I only just got him back and—"

Irritation sharpened my tone. "You got him back? *You* didn't get anything, Jilyana. He was mine."

She stared at me in wide-eyed horror. "Oh, no. I didn't mean it like that. I just...I meant that I only just found him again and..." She sighed in exasperation. "I'm not explaining myself very well."

I needed her help. I should back off. But the woman inside me who'd lost the man she loved refused to be silenced. "I'm not stupid, Jilyana. I saw the way you looked at him. Maybe you thought that in time you'd be able to win him back." She blinked sharply, the nuances in her expression telling me that I'd hit the nail on the head. "But you'd have been wasting your time. Shem was mine. You had your chance, and you fucked it up. You broke him, so put your tears away and focus on redemption."

She tucked her chin in for several beats, making it impossible to read her expression. “You’re right. Maybe I did hope. Maybe I…It doesn’t matter now. He’s gone, and we have to focus on keeping these people safe and maybe finding another way to fix the relic.” She looked up, her gaze soft with regret. “I want to help. That’s all I want now.”

“Good, because there’s been a development. I know where the fourth piece of the relic is, and I need you to help me get it.”

Her eyes lit up. “Where? Where is it?”

“It’s in Gehenna.” I filled her in on my dream, leaving out Lucifer altogether and simply telling her that I’d seen the location. “There’s a doorway to Gehenna somewhere close by. Either in the church or around it somewhere. We need to find it.”

Her brow furrowed. “How do you know that?”

“The knowledge came to me in the dream.” Which wasn’t a lie.

She nodded. “Yes, this place has a strange energy to it. I’ve felt it ever since I got here.” She glanced at the altar. “It’s strongest here. In this area.”

“You think the doorway is here?” I stared at the area around the altar, half expecting a door to materialize.

“I don’t know…I think…I think the relic piece inside me is sensing something. The feeling might be amplified if I had the other pieces. I assume you know where they are, otherwise, you wouldn’t be trying to find the fourth piece.”

The plan had been to find the doorway then get the other two relic pieces, but if the doorway couldn’t be found without them, then… “I’ll ask Sarq to get them. Meanwhile, I need your help with something else.”

“Anything, name it.”

"I need you to help me evolve Kabiel and some of the devolved."

CHAPTER 4

BEE

The church is connected to a small cottage area with a kitchen and a dining room. I guess someone lived and worked here once. It's a tranquil looking space, which is why we chose this spot for our meeting, but right now, it's filled with sparks of anxiety and fear as voices rise to be heard above one another, everyone speaking at once.

We anticipated this reaction to our news and are ready for it.

"Enough!" Mira snaps. "Listen to me. Hey!"

A child begins to cry, and Sissy steps forward. "Stop it! Stop it, all of you. You're frightening the children."

But it isn't just the children that are frightened, and that's the problem. It was one thing running from the mall to come here because everyone knew this was the safe zone. They knew we needed one big trip to get to a new home, but now...now we're telling them that this home is no longer safe. They've barely gotten their feet under the table, and we're yanking them away, telling them that we have another journey ahead of us. A three-day trek through monster-infested territory with no known safe zones except the possibility of sanctuary at the end.

A possibility only, because we aren't sure whether base zero will even let us in, let alone house all of us.

We are offering these people a promise we may not be able to keep, and they know it.

"What if this base turns us away?" Henry asks. "What if they don't have room for more people? Resources are scarce."

I'm ready for this question. "We'll be bringing watchers with us, which means protection, and scouts to get more resources. We'll also be bringing news from Gabriel and hope for an end to all of this."

"*If* we make it," Sissy says. "It's about three days on foot. You said we don't even know if there'll be places to rest safely overnight."

"The watchers will find us places," Mira says with confidence.

"You can't be sure of that," Patrick says. His eyes are dull and his tone flat. "You can't be certain of anything going forward though, can you? Our hope...Shem...He's gone."

"Rue will find a way to fix it," Mira says. "She can still find the relic pieces and—"

"And what?" Patrick's tone is now filled with challenge. "What can she do, huh?"

This is the moment when the truth should be revealed about Rue's ability, Lucifer, all of it. But we've agreed on caution. On keeping this information to ourselves in case the Dominion get their hands on us. We can't risk them finding out our plans, but damn, it's difficult to stay quiet.

"She'll do her best," Mira says firmly, hands on hips.

"You want us to simply hope?" Sissy argues.

"Why not?" Mira retorts. "It's gotten us this far."

Everyone starts to speak at once again, and Mira's shoulders droop. She's exhausted, and I'm not surprised.

I'm done with this. They need to be given their options. Bluntly. "Enough! These are the facts, and you can do with them what you want." Silence greets me, so I continue. "Rue is going after the fourth piece of the relic. *That* is non-negotiable. To do that, she has to open a doorway, a convergence that's housed somewhere in this church. Once she does that, then this place may not be safe any longer. We don't know for sure, but it seems logical based on the information that we have. So you can either come with us to a place we know is secure and hope they let us in, or you can stay here alone and hope that it remains inaccessible to monsters. The choice is yours. No one will force you to leave here if you don't want to."

Silence greets me once more, but this time it's heavy with the weight of responsibility. Responsibility that I've handed back to everyone by giving them this choice. The choice of what to do with their lives.

"We leave at dawn. If you want to come, then pack your things and meet me by the doors when the sun comes up."

I give Mira a nod, and she trails me out of the room.

Conversation breaks out as soon as we close the door. Mira stares at it, looking as if she's tempted to go back in.

"Don't." I lightly touch her arm. "They need to make this decision themselves, each and every one of them. We don't have the luxury or resources to be dragging any reluctant party across the wastelands. This way, anyone who agrees to come will make the effort to keep their own asses alive."

"I know," she says. "I just hope...I just hope they make the right choice."

"Are you having doubts about leaving?"

"No." She smiles up at me with tired eyes. "Leaving is the wise move. I just...I'm just so tired."

"Me too. How about we make a deal? While out there, I watch your back and you watch mine."

A little light enters her tired eyes. "I'd like that. I'd like that a lot."

Sarq appears through a door at the other end of the corridor. "Bee, can I borrow you for a moment please?"

"Sure, what's up?" I join him.

"I need to retrieve the relic Shemyaza hid here, and I'll need your help to do it."

CHAPTER 5

RUE

After leaving Sarq with instructions to retrieve the relic fragments, Jilyana and I headed out of the church and across the road to the forest.

"This is dangerous," Jilyana said. "Opening the channel could attract monsters or any nearby celestials."

"I doubt celestials will be a problem, and if any monsters are drawn to us, they won't be able to get to us. We'll make sure to retreat onto the church grounds."

She was quiet for a moment before asking, "What do you need me to do?"

"Back in the city, you were able to channel the power and use it to take down the herald's claw, but this time I need you to ground me. The relic inside you is connected to the Morningstar power, so I'm hoping that with you close by, I will be able to access a huge boost of energy in a short space of time without doing too much damage to myself."

I'd done it on road to the church when I'd healed Shem, but healing and evolving were two separate things, and my gut warned me that I wouldn't walk away from this task unscathed without Jilyana and the relic inside her acting as an anchor.

"I'll do what I can," she said. "I can divert some of your power through me and the relic to split it into two streams."

"Yes, that will work. Thank you."

She fell silent as we ducked into the canopy of trees. A prickle of awareness skated over my skin, and my pulse quickened in warning, a natural response to a threat—except the threat hidden in these woods was on my side.

"Kabiel, we need to talk."

The leaves above rustled, and Jilyana moved closer to me, her hand shooting out to grab my arm.

"It's all right. They won't hurt us."

The shadows ahead parted to reveal Kabiel. "I don't have the answers you want, Rue. Not yet. No visions, despite your most generous donation last night."

"I don't need a vision. I know where the fourth relic shard is."

Disbelief and a hint of suspicion narrowed his eyes. "How? How can you know that?"

"I dreamed it. It's in Gehenna."

Soft chitters filled the air around me, and a sense of panic bloomed in the atmosphere. Why were the devolved panicking?

"Silence!" Kabiel snapped, then to me, "You're a fool coming here to deliver such news. Hope is all that is keeping my watchers tethered, and you come here to take that away?"

What? Wait...He thought hope was lost? Shit, he didn't know there was a way to get into Gehenna. "No, Kabiel. You don't understand. The relic fragment *is* in Gehenna, but we can go after it. There's a doorway to Gehenna in the church.

I plan to open it and go through, and I want...No, I *need* you and some of your watchers to come with me."

"Monsters to fight the monsters you may encounter, *hmmmm*?"

I lifted my chin. "You won't be so much of a monster when I'm done with you."

He scanned my face. "You hope to get us into the church. It would take a vast injection of Morningstar power to achieve that goal."

But there was longing in his tone. Longing and pure hope.

"I can do it with Jilyana's help. I can evolve you enough to get you through the church and into Gehenna."

Soft chitters echoed around us as the devolved absorbed this information.

"Pick your troop, Kabiel. I won't be able to evolve everyone, so pick wisely. The rest will have residual power to feed off during the channeling."

His nostrils flared, and he stepped back, the tips of his spider legs sinking into the earth and making no sound.

"I would choose you all if I could," Kabiel said. "But I cannot. My brothers, you have fought valiantly against the growing darkness. Fight a little longer, and powers that be willing, we will once again find the light."

I hated this. Hated that I couldn't help them all, but my ability had limits, even with Jilyana's help.

Kabiel took a moment, his gaze blank as he looked inward. When he spoke, his tone was studded with authority. "Asbeel, Kokabel, Yomiel, and Matarel, you will join me."

Four devolved emerged from between the trees, just as large as Kabiel and slightly more devolved-looking than he was, but each looked humanoid enough that I was sure I could get them to a state where the wards on the church wouldn't hold them back.

Jilyana took my hand and gave me a nod, letting me know she was ready when I was.

"Gather around." I stepped closer to Kabiel. "Gather close."

Kabiel put his arm around me, drawing Jilyana closer in the process. She tensed, and I squeezed her hand to let her know it was okay.

The other four devolved moved in so that we were surrounded by them. The rest remained hidden in the shadowy canopy above.

I pressed my palm to Kabiel's pectoral. "Jilyana?"

She hesitated before pressing her palm to his other pectoral.

I looked up at the watcher. "Are you ready?"

His silvery gaze skipped over my features, lingering on my lips before locking on to my eyes. "Yes, Rue. I am ready. We are ready."

I closed my eyes and reached deep into myself to open the door to the Morningstar power. Lucifer's power. It blasted into me with such force that my back arched and my eyes snapped open. Kabiel stared at me, stunned, his mouth a soft 'o' that was quickly obscured by white-hot blazing power.

Jilyana's grip on my hand bordered on painful as we held the connection for achingly long seconds until my lungs were too tight to breathe and my eyes sizzled in their sockets.

Enough.

Now was enough.

I squeezed my eyes closed, found the door, and pushed. The last time I'd been too weak to close it alone, but with

Jilyana helping me to channel the power, I had enough strength to slam it closed.

It cut off, and my knees buckled. Jilyana's hand slipped out of mine, but Kabiel's hold on me tightened so that I was pressed to him, cheek against the very pectoral I'd just had my palm against a moment ago.

"I've got you, Rue." His voice sounded different.

The gooseflesh-inducing raspy quality was gone, replaced by a smooth baritone that sent a different kind of shiver up my spine.

I blinked away the dark spots in my vision, pushing away from him so I could inspect my handiwork. It took a moment for my vision to clear, but when it did, I wasn't sure if my eyes were playing tricks on me, because the male standing before me was so far removed from the devolved watcher that it was difficult to reconcile the two.

This version of Kabiel had silver hair streaked with black. His eyes, silvery gray with flecks of blue, were framed by thick, dark lashes. His face was still angular with a sharp jaw and high cheekbones, but his lips were fuller...softer, and the biggest change, the one that told me that I might have pulled this off, was the reduction of his spider legs. Only two remained, jutting out of his back beneath his wings. The rest were gone, allowing him to stand firmly on his feet.

He turned his hands over and ran them down his chest, twisting his body to look over his shoulder, examining himself.

"She did it," one of the other watchers said. His dark hair was shorn close to his scalp, and his features were broader, his frame stockier. "You did it." He beamed at me, showcasing blunt white teeth.

"But it won't last, Asbeel. Not unless we fix the relic,"

another one of the watchers said. He had messy sandy hair and a leaner build.

"You're right, Yomiel," Kabiel said. "We need to make this gift count."

He fixed his beautiful silver eyes on me. "We're ready. Let's find this door and get to Gehenna."

I needed to tell him the full story about Lucifer, but not with Jilyana present. "Jilyana, why don't you go back to the church and find Sarq. See if you can locate the door. We'll join you in a few minutes."

She nodded quickly and backed away, looking more than eager to be out of the forest and away from the shivering trees.

I waited until she was visible by the picket fence that surrounded the church before turning to Kabiel. "There's more you need to know."

He slow-blinked. "I thought as much. Tell me everything."

CHAPTER 6

BEE

The basement is accessed through a door set beneath the stairs. It's a cramped space, and Sarq struggles to fit his large, stocky frame inside and pull up the hatch in the floor.

"Let me?" I slip past him and fall into a crouch to get at the door. It sticks for a moment before coming free, and the distinct smell of mildew hits me.

A set of stone steps descend into darkness beyond. "It's dark. We might need a flashlight."

"One moment." Sarq rummages on a shelf behind me. "Here." He hands me a flashlight. "It should be wound."

We had these at base too—flashlights that worked on kinetic energy. I switch it on, and a beam of light cuts through the darkness below. It's not a wide stairwell, and for a moment I'm worried that Sarq won't be able to fit, but he manages to squeeze down the hatch, taking up the rear as we descend.

Dark shapes loom around us—boxes covered with tarp

and old furniture stored away, dusty and covered in cobwebs.

Once I'm on the concrete floor, I move away from the steps to let Sarq down. The scrape of a match is followed by the bloom of warm light that illuminates a large circumference of space.

I shut off the flashlight in favor of Sarq's lamp. He takes the lead across the room, past a box filled with books and magazines wrapped in plastic. I make a note to come back and browse the literature. Maybe pick one book to take with me on our journey.

"The relics are in the chest," Sarq says. "Shem purposefully warded it against celestials, and that includes watchers. Only a mortal can open it."

"He planned for Rue to do this, didn't he?"

"Yes."

The chest looks mundane. No glowing runes. Nothing to make it stand out. Clever. But there is no mistaking the fizz of energy when I reach out to touch it. There's power coating the object. I unclasp and lift the lid to reveal odd moth-eaten clothes.

"Underneath," Sarq says.

A moment of rummaging and my fingers graze something cold and smooth. I pull out the curved piece of metal? Ceramic? I can't tell what material this is, but then, it's probably no earthly material.

The second piece is just as large. It's impossible to tell what the object they originally made must look like.

"What is it?" I hold up the pieces. "What is the Morningstar relic? What does it look like?"

"It doesn't have a set form," Sarq says. "From what Shemyaza told me, the object could change, almost as if it were alive."

"If it's a part of Lucifer, a part of her soul, I suppose it is. But it's inert now." I'm not sure why that makes me feel sad. I wrap the fragments in a blanket from the chest.

"They can't break," Sarq says. "Turns out only Shemyaza had the power to damage the relic."

As soon as he says this, it hits me that this is a question that has been bugging me. "Rue said Shemyaza was supposed to be the messenger, right? He was meant to go take the Morningstar to Lucifer when it was time for her to be free."

"That would seem so."

"Because this Morningstar relic was important to God. To keeping the fabric of the worlds intact."

"Yes. I'm not sure where you're going with this line of thought..."

"Why make anyone able to fracture it, then?"

Sarq frowns. "I...I'm not sure."

"Yeah, it doesn't make sense to me either." I pull myself to my feet and tuck the wrapped relic pieces beneath my arm. "Maybe Rue can ask Lucifer once she gets to Gehenna."

"What does it matter now? Shemyaza is gone." He turns away. "Come. Let's get the relics to Rue."

His sadness is a palpable force that leads me back up the steps and out of the basement. You'd think nothing could hurt these huge, hulking males, but they're hurting right now.

Shem's sacrifice won't be for nothing. The bastard Dominion will pay, and Michael...I hope I have a front row seat when that traitorous fucker gets taken down.

I'm closing the hatch when a shrill scream shatters the relative silence.

Sarq hauls me to my feet, and we run toward the sound,

coming to a halt by the cloak room between the kitchen and the study. People are gathered outside.

Someone is crying.

"Out of the way!" Sarq demands.

People stagger away, hands on mouths, eyes wide as they tear their gazes from the scene in the cloak room.

Patrick hangs from a beam. I'm not sure where he found the rope. It hardly matters.

He's dead.

Sarq exhales sharply then quickly moves to cut him down, but I'm rooted to the spot, pulse pounding in my throat. This is my fault because I gave him two options—stay and risk being eaten by monsters or come with us and *maybe* not be eaten by monsters.

Patrick found a third option.

CHAPTER 7

RUE

We laid Patrick to rest in the cemetery behind the church at dawn. Sissy said a few words, but mostly everyone was silent and subdued.

In a world filled with monsters, death was nothing new, and the last few months had brought more than our fair share, but this...This kind of death weighed heavily on us all. Should we have known? Should we have seen?

Was this my fault? If I'd told them the truth...taken the risk, would he be alive today?

It was all I could think about when I should be focused on finding and opening the door to Gehenna.

The relic pieces sat on the desk, wrapped in a blanket, ready for me. Mira was ushering people to the nave in preparation for their trek.

Things were moving forward despite the tragedy, but guilt held me captive.

"Hey?" Bee entered the study and closed the door behind her. "Jilyana's asking for you."

"Do you think I should tell everyone...everything?"

Bee sighed. "No." She walked over to the boarded-up window and parked her ass on the sill. "I admit, when we found Patrick, I thought...I wondered, but, Rue, this isn't about one person's life. This is about everyone. About the whole fucking world. If we do tell them and the Dominion get hold of us, then they'll find out about Lucifer and the doorway and the fragments. Everything. We can't take that risk, and Patrick...Even if we'd told him, he'd still have been faced with the same two options. Patrick was done. We can sit here speculating and pointing fingers and wondering what if, but it won't change the fact that he's gone, and we still have a bunch of people out there waiting for us to save them." She walked over and took my hands in hers. "We can protect them from the monsters out there, but only they can fight the monsters within."

Bee and her wisdom would forever be my anchor. "I love you, you know that?"

"Yeah." She grabbed my face and planted a sloppy kiss on my forehead. "Love you too. Now let's get out there and get this show on the road. Kabiel and his troop arrived a few minutes ago, and everyone's a little freaked out."

I stared at her in shock. "Why didn't you lead with that?"

She shrugged. "You needed a moment. Now you've had it."

I grabbed the relic bundle and followed her out of the door. Yep, Bee always seemed to know what I needed to hear, and I loved her for it.

THE NAVE of the church was lined not only with pews but with people staring at Kabiel and his team. My injection of celestial power had removed most of their spider-like appearance, but compared to the watchers that these people were used to, Kabiel and his team were still monstrous.

They stood in a lose arrowhead formation with Kabiel at the tip, wings tucked tightly against his back. His two spider legs were also contracted close to his body so that all his weight was on his feet. Bare feet, larger than normal and covered in thick crimson skin.

If they minded being the center of attention, they didn't show it. In fact, they all looked perfectly at ease eating up space with their larger-than-life frames, deep in conversation with Gabriel, Erelim, and Bastian.

I approached the group, and they broke off their chat and turned to me.

"Kabiel, I was going to come find you once we'd located the door."

"Now you don't need to," he said with a tense smile. "We can leave as soon as you open it."

He was worried that the effects of the Morningstar power would wear off, and I wasn't about to question him. He understood his body better than me.

"I was just telling Kabiel about our most recent loss," Gabriel said smoothly.

"I'm very sorry to hear what happened," Kabiel said. "But we cannot hold off much longer."

"I know. We're going to find the door now, but we can't activate it or pass through it until everyone has left, just in case doing so drops the wards on this place."

Bastian sucked in a breath. "It's all happening so fast now."

Erelim placed a hand on Bastian's shoulder. "The quicker they leave, the quicker they can return. Time will move fast once we're on the road."

But Bastian's gaze, locked with mine, filled with shadows of fear and doubt. There was nothing more I could say or do to assuage his reservations, and if I tried, I was afraid that I might become infected by his doubts.

No. I needed to act now.

I searched the crowd for Jilyana and found her standing closest to the altar. "I have the relic pieces." I passed her the bundle.

She hugged it to her chest and closed her eyes. "Yes, I feel the power."

"Can you use it to find the convergence?"

She walked the short distance to the altar and fixed me with a triumphant look. "I knew there was a reason I was drawn to this spot. The door is here. Right here, and now I can feel how strong the energy is." She reached out with trembling fingers to touch the altar. "We have to move this somehow."

Bastian joined her at the altar and began to examine it.

"There's a seam here, but that doesn't mean it can be moved." He gave the structure a shove. "It also doesn't mean that it can't." He ran his fingers over the surface of the altar, then along the edge of the counter and beneath. "Ah...I think..."

Click.

A soft rumbling sound filled the air, and the altar slid back to reveal a three-by-three aperture and a set of steps.

"Yes!" Jilyana hugged the relic bundle to her chest. "It's down there." She slipped down the steps before I could stop her.

"Wait!" I hurried after her, and Bastian followed.

The gloom lit up an eerie green color as a strange growth on the walls began to glow, as if activated by our presence.

"What is that?" Bastian said.

"I don't know."

"The power..." Jilyana crooned. "It's calling to me."

The steps seemed to go on forever as we descended into the earth for what felt like minutes but surely couldn't have been that long.

A new source of light filtered up the steps, and the green glow died.

"Almost there." Jilyana's voice trembled with excitement.

The bottom of the steps came into view—flagstones decorated with strange etchings.

Jilyana led the way away from the steps and through an arch into a circular chamber that housed a well.

"There!" She leaned over the edge. "Oh...It's...beautiful."

It looked like she was about to topple in, so I grabbed her and hauled her away. "What are you doing?"

She yanked her arm away from me with a frown. "What are *you* doing? It's the door. We must go through it."

I grabbed her again, but she was strong and broke free, making a leap toward the well, but Bastian managed to hook an arm around her, then Gabriel appeared, placing himself between the well and Jilyana.

"Take the relics off her," he said. "Do it now."

It took a moment, but I managed to wrestle the bundle from her and back away with it.

Jilyana stopped fighting and went still. "I...I'm sorry. I'm not sure what just happened."

"You were enraptured," Gabriel said. "It happens sometimes when a being is presented with an excess of power. Power that isn't naturally meant to flow through them."

"The relics?" Bastian said.

"The relics and this doorway..." Gabriel peered into the well. "It's ancient. This convergence...almost as if it was planned."

"And maybe it was," Kabiel said from the steps. "A hidden doorway between worlds is hardly a novelty."

"It is when God asserted that all such doors were sealed," Gabriel pointed out.

"I think the relics help to open this door," Jilyana said. "The power inside them...It's meant to open the way."

This was Lucifer's power, which meant this door was created for her. The well was large, though, at least five feet in diameter. "We'll need to go down in groups. Each group holding a relic to make sure no one gets locked out."

I inched closer to the well and looked down at the swirling red and purple portal housed inside.

"We go. Now," Kabiel said.

"As soon as the people have left. We need to give them an hour." I looked across at Bastian. "You need to go."

His throat bobbed. "I know, but I need..." He licked his lips. "I have some supplies packed for you. Food and water. You better come and make sure you have everything you might need."

I nodded mutely, my mouth suddenly dry because this was happening. The portal was here, and I was about to go to hell.

Back in the study upstairs, Bastian pulled me into his arms in a bear hug that melted my resolve to stay strong.

My eyes heated with the threat of tears. “Bastian, I’m scared. I’m so fucking scared.”

He squeezed me tight. “So am I. Dammit. I wish I could come with you. I wish you didn’t have to go.”

We remained locked in an embrace for long minutes, hearts beating in tandem, breath synchronized until a calm settled over me.

“I’m coming back, Bastian. I’m coming back, and you better be at base zero waiting for me.” I pulled away and glared up at him. “No heroics on the way. No putting your life on the line out there, because I fucking need you to live. You understand?”

He smiled wryly. “Practice what you preach much, Rue?”

“Trust me, if I didn’t have to go, then I wouldn’t.” But I was the only one who could locate the final relic fragment.

Bastian cupped my face with his large hands. “No heroics.”

I turned my face to kiss his palm. “No heroics.”

His kiss was soft and filled with emotions that made knots in my chest. But this wasn’t goodbye. This was *see you later*. It had to be.

Bastian had not only packed me a bag, as promised, but he’d also fashioned me a weapon. I’d lost my bat somewhere in our travels, but Bastian had found me another. It wasn’t bound with barbed wire, but he’d added a few nails to it for added impact. The bag contained neatly packed dried meat and cereals, a couple of bottles of water, and some of Mira’s cookies. We didn’t have a huge amount to spare, so I’d have to be prudent with the supplies and hope that there’d be water and food in Gehenna.

Nerves did the tango in my blood as we went back into the nave. Bee stepped in to give me a hug, but with the relic bundle tucked under my arm and my bat clutched in the other, I couldn't return it properly. She squeezed hard enough for us both, though, and I leaned into that, reveling in the contact and committing it to memory.

"Be safe and come back to us," she whispered into my hair before releasing me.

Baraqel dropped me a nod, and Erelim lifted his chin slightly in goodbye. Penemue and Armaros stood to one side, silent and watchful. I was leaving my people in their hands. People who stood silent and forlorn on the edges of the room.

They'd be fine.

"We'll keep them safe," Sarq said. "Give us an hour before you go through the convergence."

"Of course."

Mira hauled the door open. "Okay, everyone. Time to hit the road."

People started to trickle out into the mid-morning sun. We'd left it later than planned for them to leave, but the watchers had used that time to mark off some potential safe zones on Zaq's map.

They'd be fine.

Everything would be fine if I did my part.

The nave emptied out until it was just Bee, Bastian, and me.

They sandwiched me in a final hug, and it took everything in me not to drop the bat and relics and hold on to them as terror surged hot in my veins.

This could be the end.

It could be goodbye.

"We love you, Rue," Bee said. "We'll see you soon."

They crossed to the door and stood momentarily silhouetted in the sunlight. Then they too were gone.

I hurried back down the steps to rejoin my party in the chamber beneath the altar. We had an hour to kill, and I had no doubt that it would feel like the longest hour of my life.

CHAPTER 8

MICHAEL

The view from the pinnacle is nothing but mist and clouds, obscuring the world below. The walls of the city are visible in the distance with their many sentries flying back and forth.

This is the view I should have been given from the start.

These opulent chambers are owed to me, with the huge living area and three rooms coming off the living space for me to do with as I please. The location—a floor below the Dominion—is also ideal, indicating my elevated station.

Ending Shemyaza has saved us all. This world will be our new home, and I can't wait to put the final stages of the Dominion's plan into motion.

The knock on the main doors pulls me out of my thoughts. "Come in."

Yamal steps into the room decked out in his bronze armor, ever ready for battle. He takes in the room with economic darts of his dark eyes, and his mouth tightens a fraction.

Oh, this must be tearing him apart.

Being my subordinate and answering to me when a few short days ago he would have had the power to crush me. Now I can take away his breath with a thought. I can make him fall to his knees and beg for mercy.

But I'm above such petty actions. "What news?"

"There's been a disturbance in the ether northeast of here. An ejection of power that I believe we should investigate."

"You believe it related to our mission?"

"I believe it's worth investigating," he repeats.

He needs my permission, but I pause for long seconds, making him wait. I let him seethe, and then I shrug one shoulder. "Go. Take a small troop and investigate. Summon me if you determine the disturbance to be a viable fracture."

"As you order, Michael," Yamal says.

"You will address me by my given title." I can all but hear his teeth grinding, and the satisfaction that brings me is unparalleled.

"As you order, Supracelestia," he says stiffly.

A new title gifted to me by the Dominion, putting me above all others except them. I can live with that...for now.

Power crackles in my veins. I'm whole. A savior. A conqueror, and soon I will be much more.

CHAPTER 9

RUE

The hour ticked by faster than expected with Kabiel, his watchers, Gabriel and Jilyana for company. It was peaceful here in the bowels of the earth beneath the church surrounded by stone and earth with only each other's heartbeats for company.

The watchers swapped stories about their lives before the fall. About the wars they'd fought on God's command, about the times they'd walked among humans, and the snippets they'd heard about Gehenna.

Asbeel thought it to be a prison realm, but Yomiel said he'd heard it was the first world that God created. Matarel said that the prison realm theory was the most popular one in heaven, but no one knew for certain what the world was like.

It was clear that Gehenna was a mystery to all; even humanity had created its own stories around it—calling it hell and saying it was the place that human souls went if they did evil things.

But with the hour up, the time for speculation was over.

I handed Kabiel the bundle containing two of the relic pieces. "You and your watchers can pass through using these. Gabriel and I'll go through with Jilyana." I hoisted my pack firmly onto my shoulders and gripped my bat tightly. "Let's do this before I change my mind."

We were going into the unknown with me as the compass that would lead us to the relic piece, and after that, we'd have to wing it.

The well lip wasn't too high, so it was easy to climb onto the ledge. The portal swirled brighter as if sensing the relic inside Jilyana.

I shoved my bat into my pack the best I could before linking hands with Gabriel and Jilyana. "See you on the other side, Kabiel."

We jumped.

The lights went out for a moment, and when they flared back on, my boots were on rocky ground. An angry red sky swirling with purple clouds stretched out above us like a frothy blanket. My hands were still clasped with Jilyana and Gabriel, who both looked as disorientated as I felt. Were their chests as tight as mine?

Where were Kabiel and his team?

I scanned the gray, rocky landscape that stretched out around us, but there was no sign of them. Was that a drop a few meters ahead of us?

The air crackled, and Kabiel and his team materialized a little to our left in various versions of a crouch. Kabiel's gaze instantly found me, locking on like a homing beacon. I raised a hand to let him know I was good.

But where was the doorway we'd come through? There was no visible sign of it on this side. Shit.

Gabriel squeezed my hand, turning me to face him. “Rue? Are you all right? You’re breathing fast.”

Now that he mentioned it, yeah, I was having a little trouble with my breathing, and it had nothing to do with panic. Maybe the journey had affected me? Maybe it was the air here? “I’ll be fine.”

“What’s wrong with her?” Kabiel demanded, almost accusingly.

Gabriel’s frown was the only indication that Kabiel’s tone irked him. “I’m not sure.” His emerald eyes narrowed, and he gently pressed his fingers to the pulse at my throat. “Your heart is having to work harder here. It would be dangerous for you to exert yourself.” Then to Kabiel, “The atmosphere isn’t optimal for her.”

Kabiel growled softly as he scanned our surroundings. “The doorway is nowhere to be seen. We can’t take her back.”

Even if the door was here, I wouldn’t go back. “I’m fine.”

I’d considered that the atmosphere might be less than perfect for my biology, but Lucifer had asked me to come, and surely she wouldn’t have done that if she thought I’d die along the way. “I’m sure I’ll acclimatize.”

“Or you could die,” Kabiel said. “There could be toxins in the air that slowly kill you.”

Gabriel shot him a hard look that clearly said *seriously?*

“She should be aware of the risks,” Kabiel continued. “We move fast. Get this done and get her out of this place.”

I had to agree. “But which way do we go?”

“Can you feel the relic?” Kabiel asked. “Did Shem teach you how to scry for it?”

“He told me, but we never had a chance to put the theory into practice.” My heart sank. “I’ll try now.”

We had no idea where in Gehenna we were, but if we

were close to the relic, scrying for it would tell me. I closed my eyes and reached for the door inside me. But instead of opening it, I pressed my hands to it first, allowing the residue of the power to infuse my phantom palms and asking it for its guidance. *Help me find you. Draw me to you.* I cracked open the door to the Morningstar a teeny fraction and focused on the vibration of power inside.

Shem had explained how I could use it to pinpoint the location of a relic, but we'd never done so in practice. Kabiel had been our locator for each one. But this time, I focused on the vibration, asking it to guide me to the parts that made it whole.

A tingle of acknowledgement passed through me and then a hard tug drew me to my left, then to my right, then left again until my body was torn.

What the fuck? My eyes snapped open to Jilyana's face. Jilyana, who had a relic piece inside her, and to my right stood Kabiel with the bundle containing the other two relic pieces.

"This isn't going to be easy with relics around me already."

"I'm sorry," she said. "I'll shield the relic inside me first, and you hand me the other two. I might be able to shield them too." She held out her hands to Kabiel, but the watcher ignored her and looked to me.

We'd spoken about my suspicions, and he was waiting for permission to give her the precious fragments.

Jilyana exhaled softly, her expression weary and wry. "You don't trust me. I understand that, but if we're going to survive in this place, then you need to give me the benefit of the doubt."

She was right; if we were going to get through this and find the final piece, then we'd have to trust her to help us.

Besides, we were in Gehenna now, and if she planned to betray us and run off with the relics, she wouldn't get far.

"It's okay, Kabiel. Give Jilyana the relics for now."

Kabiel handed her the bundle, and she hugged it to her chest looking across at me with such warm gratitude that it made me feel like an absolute shit for doubting her.

"Let me see if I can hide them," she said. A strange hum filled the air, and the hairs on my body quivered. "Try scrying now."

I took a deep breath and repeated the steps. This time, there was no tingle of awareness, no awakening, which meant that Jilyana had succeeded in hiding the relics. It also meant that we weren't close enough to the fourth relic for the power to pick up on it.

I released my hold on the power and opened my eyes. "We're nowhere close to the relic piece."

"Then we get moving," Kabiel said. "You can scry at various intervals."

"What about you?" Gabriel asked Jilyana. "Can you help find the relic piece, considering you have one inside you? Will you sense when the other one is close?"

"I…I don't know. I couldn't find the pieces in the church."

"You were searching for them?" Kabiel's tone was sharp.

Her eyes flew wide. "No. I mean…I didn't sense anything. Not until Rue brought them to me." She looked to me. "I wasn't searching for anything. Honest."

It wouldn't have mattered anyway. "They were hidden by runes at the church."

She dropped her gaze. "Yes, that would explain it."

"So can you help locate the relic pieces?" Gabriel asked.

She shrugged a shoulder. "I suppose so. I suppose I might be able to sense if they were near."

She could be a compass just like me. But then, had it

been necessary for me to come? No, Lucifer had asked *me* to do this. To complete the task Shem would have done.

"We can always use the extra help," Gabriel said with a tight smile. "You'll let us know if you sense the relic piece." It wasn't a request.

"Of course," Jilyana said. "I'm here to help. To atone."

Dammit, were we being too hard on her? Every word out of her mouth was saturated with a sincerity that made it hard to doubt her.

"Let's get moving," Gabriel said. "We'll check the drop first."

"Be on guard," Kabiel said to his team, then to Gabriel, "We'll lead."

The watchers moved forward, and Gabriel took my hand once more, his fingers warm and firm around mine.

There was indeed a dip ahead. Not just a dip, but a huge bowl cut into the rocky terrain that stretched out into the distance and had to be at least a hundred feet deep. But it was the contents of the bowl that drew my attention—red and orange swaying fleshy projections that looked like they were alive. They reminded me of something I'd seen in a book on biology a long time ago, the tiny projections that jutted out of cells...Cilia. Yes, the bowl was filled with thousands upon thousands of cilia swaying in a phantom breeze.

"What is that?" Matarel asked in a hushed voice. "They're alive?"

"Yes," Jilyana said. "They are, and they all have an aura... So many auras."

Something else moved within the bowl. A shadow...a silhouette. No. It was a large serpentine creature, cutting a zig-zag path through the projections, which parted to let it through.

"Do you see that?" Jilyana asked.

The serpent came to a halt in its meandering and slowly turned its body to point in our direction before raising its worm-like head.

It was far below us, but there was no doubt in my mind that it had seen us.

"It's spotted us." Gabriel's grip on me tightened, and tension spiked the air. "Back away. Slowly."

The flutter in my chest was now also in my head. I grabbed Gabriel's arm to steady myself just as the serpent leapt from the pit.

Right at us.

CHAPTER 10

The serpent arched toward us, growing larger by the second.

Kabiel yelled a warning, and Gabriel shoved me with his whole frame, desperate to get us out from under the serpent's shadow.

Jilyana screamed.

The serpent vanished mid-flight.

"Where did it go?" Asbeel demanded as if we'd have the answers.

A deep masculine voice spoke from behind us. "Visitors. How wonderful."

We spun to face the speaker—a tall, slender male with dark hooded eyes and a lopsided smile. His clothes were made of shadows that floated around his frame, and his skin was as white as bone.

He looked dead and yet he exuded life. It pulsed around him, hugging his frame lovingly.

Wait...was I seeing an aura? Was that the energy that surrounded him?

Kabiel and his watchers surged forward to flank us. But Jilyana seemed unfazed.

"You have no aura," she said to the man.

Okay, so what the hell *was* I seeing?

"And yours blazes with regret and indecision," he said to her. "What is it you fight?"

Jilyana's throat bobbed. "Everyone has inner demons."

"I do not. But then I suppose that is one of the advantages of being a god."

"You are *not* God," Gabriel said. "I would know if you were."

"Would you?" The creature's eyes were hidden so deep in their sockets that it was hard to tell who he was looking at, but there was a focused energy about him which was now directed at Gabriel.

Was this God? "Gabriel?"

"This isn't God," Gabriel said firmly. "I would feel it if he was."

The creature snorted, an indelicate sound that held the edge of bitter amusement. "Yes, of course you would; you are, after all, created from *his* being. But you should pay more attention to words spoken. I did not claim to *be* God. I claimed to be *a* god. There are many of us, contrary to what *your* god may have wanted you to believe. The term *god* is a generic one. He simply chose to claim it as his name." He canted his head to the side. "Which means that you come from one of his worlds. He was never one to share. But this place belongs to us all. We created it together. Our first world. Our first home. After which...Well, I've lost count."

"Who *are* you?" Gabriel demanded.

"I have many names on many worlds," the god said. "Hades, Anubis, Erebus, and most commonly, Death. But in this world, I am called Thanatos." He drifted forward, and an icy chill washed over me. "This world belongs to the old gods. We may leave and enter at will or invite a guest to roam here. But it is unlike him to invite guests here."

Did he realize this place was fractured? No. From the way he was talking, he had no clue the danger we were in. "We're not guests of anyone, especially not God. We're here because there are fractures in the fabric of my world, and monsters from *this* world have come through. We're on a mission to try and re-establish a balance."

"Fractures, you say? Escaped...*monsters*?" His mouth turned down. "There are no monsters here. Only Gehenna-born beings."

"They're monsters to my people. Killing them, hunting them."

"Ah, the cycle of life. Necessary for the survival of any biosphere. But yes...I suppose it might upset the balance of your world." He blinked sharply. "It seems I have wandered for too long this time. I should have returned sooner to check..." He tipped his head to the side and closed his eyes for several long beats. "Yes. The fringes are fractured, and the first creations are in danger." His eyes snapped open. "This is unacceptable. He vowed to us that he would never let his creations encroach on our collective haven."

He? "Do you mean God?"

"Yes. Your god."

"You're saying that we're encroaching?" Anger spawned in my chest. "How many humans, aside from me, do you see traipsing around this world?"

"Humans...so volatile," he drawled. "When I say creations, I mean worlds. Your world is his creation, and it's obviously encroaching on Gehenna. Mortals are *his* playthings, and he enjoys designing arenas for them to inhabit." He shook his head in obvious disgust. "The messes he's made, and now this..." He exhaled though his nose. "The Morningstar has been compromised, hasn't it?"

"How do you know about that?" Gabriel asked.

"I helped forge the damned thing. Helped create the messenger, Shemyaza. The first watcher, which your god then used to create more. Watchers...Creatures who could feed on Lucifer's energy, *not* on your god's. But you are not Shemyaza." He peered into my soul with his dark eye sockets that reminded me of twin voids. "No, you are not him, and yet...Yet you are." He shook his head. "If the Morningstar has been compromised, then we are running out of time. Lucifer will need to be made aware and—"

"The Morningstar shattered two decades ago." This creature might be able to help us, and we needed to get him up to speed quickly. "And Lucifer already knows. I spoke to her in a dream. She asked me to bring the relic pieces to her."

He took a step forward. "You have them?"

Jilyana shrank away from him, her grip on the bundle of relics tightening, and it hit me that she now knew our full mission. From the annoyed look on Gabriel's face, he'd realized it too.

Thanatos's head whipped toward her. "*You* have them. You shield well, little fireling, but you cannot fool a god."

"We don't have them all," Gabriel said. "There's one in the fifth circle of this place."

"The fifth?" His brows shot up. "Ah, then you will have a challenge ahead of you. This rocky terrain that houses my many fields of souls is in the seventh circle. You must pass through the sixth to reach your destination." He winced. "The sixth belongs to a god that does not take kindly to interlopers. In fact, she abhors them."

We could fight monsters, but I doubted we'd be able to

fight a god. "Can't you come with us to pass through the sixth?"

"I'm afraid not. Zeus barred me from her circle after an incident that occurred some time ago. She isn't the most forgiving of gods. Maybe you'll be lucky and find her absent, in which case, all you need do is bypass the guardian that lives in the chasm between the two circles. Time your passage and you won't be interrupted."

"And the fifth? Who rules the fifth?" Gabriel asked.

"The fifth is a circle of water ruled by Dione, but she long abandoned it. There isn't much land to speak of any longer, but you may be able to get assistance from the inhabitants of that circle."

"And the rest?" Gabriel asked. "The circles leading to Lucifer?"

"Are in her domain. I'm sure she'll find you when the time is right. I wish I could do more. This world holds a special place in my heart, and if it bleeds into another, then both worlds will eventually die. But death is a part of life." He waved an arm toward the crater of souls. "And we must accept the natural order of things. If this world is to end, then so be it."

That was bullshit. "You're a god. You're supposed to be able to control such things."

He snorted again, but this time, the sound held no humor. "And where did you learn that? In a book detailing the responsibilities of gods? There is no such text. There is no list. We are creators. We are raw power. We are endless." His eyes dimmed. "Doomed to watch the birth and death of the stars, our only consolation lies in the small pockets of life we create among them. Worlds woven together by intricate threads so that they sit in a web so complex that even we struggle to trace the patterns. Sometimes we create together, watch over the worlds in union, and others we prefer to go alone." A whisper of a sigh escaped his lips. "This world, our first, is dear to my heart, and the fact that you are here gives me hope for its survival. But only you can realize it. I will transport you to the edge of my domain, but I can take you no further. Will you accept my aid?"

Everything he said felt true. And any help he could give would be appreciated. "We'll accept your help." My words came out breathless, and a wave of dizziness assaulted as the world darkened.

Gabriel caught my weight, helping me to remain upright. "Rue!" He patted my cheek, and I forced my eyes open.

"I'm okay."

"No. You are not," Thanatos said. "This world is not for mortals, and your body, although not entirely human, is being affected by the atmosphere." He pressed his lips together as if considering something. "May I assist you?"

I felt like there was a bear sitting on my chest. "Go for it."

He touched my forehead with icy fingers, and the chill spread outward from the contact, gripping my head with frosty talons. The weight on my chest eased, allowing my lungs to swell on a satisfied breath.

"There," Thanatos said. "I've adjusted you enough to allow your body to process this atmosphere."

"Thank you." I pressed my hand to my breastbone. "I feel better."

Gabriel smoothed the hair back from my face. "You have some color in your cheeks too." His smile was soft with relief as his hand dropped to my throat, fingers curling around my neck to press against my pulse. My stomach flipped and my breath caught. "Your pulse is steady." His tone was slightly lower now, and when I met his eyes, his pupils were dark and large.

Energy pulsed between us. Our bond. Our connection. I pulled away from him. "I'm good. Thanks." His expression shuttered, and I was glad.

There were boundaries between us. He needed to remember that.

"How far is it to the border of your territory?" Kabiel asked Thanatos.

"A few hundred miles," Thanatos said. "Just beyond the small settlement of Gehennans that help to watch over my souls."

"There are people here?"

"Like humans, Gehennans, too, come in various sizes, colors, and temperaments. The inhabitants of my circle are a private bunch, and they do not like outsiders. Luckily, there is little need for them to leave, and we do not get many visitors from other circles. The path to the seventh can be trying for some."

"What do you mean?"

"I'll explain once we get to the gate."

"You lead, and we can fly," Kabiel said.

"You could, but I would advise saving your energy for the sixth circle. Let me carry you." He vanished and a moment later appeared in his serpent form a few feet away from us. He was an impressive beast, with shimmering obsidian scales and a body that sat over five feet off the ground and goodness only knew how long.

"You may mount me," he said.

I shrugged my pack off and held it out to Jilyana. "Do you want to use it to hold the relics? It'll mean keeping hold of my supplies."

"It's the least I can do," she said.

I waited for her to ask about Lucifer, but she didn't. I'd have to clear the air with her later.

We quickly made the transfer before Gabriel flew me up onto Thanatos's back. We settled in a straddle position, putting me between Gabriel's thighs, and I was surprised at how natural it felt to be sitting so intimately with the celestial.

Jilyana dithered below us.

"What is it?" Gabriel called out. "Are you afraid?"

"No, I just...I can't seem to teleport. I tried earlier when Thanatos leapt out of the pit, but it didn't work then either."

"Come." Asbeel held out his arms to her, and after a moment's hesitation, Jilyana stepped into them. He flew up and landed somewhere behind us. The other watchers followed.

Kabiel took a spot in front of us but didn't straddle the serpent. Instead, he crouched, spider legs holding on to the creature's scaly body.

"Hold on," Thanatos said.

The next moment, the world around us disintegrated into a blur.

We were moving so fast it was impossible for my eyes to track the terrain without feeling nauseous, so I tucked in my chin and leaned into Gabriel, focusing on the solid form of his body around me. With his inner thighs pressed to my hips, his arms around my waist, and his heat beating against my back, the effects of the rapid motion soon ebbed, allowing me to sink into myself as the rolling nausea in my belly dissipated.

I was all right.

"Almost there," Thanatos said. "Just a little way—"

Our ride came to a jarring halt that yanked me out of Gabriel's arms and flung me into the air. My scream lodged in my throat, eyes flying wide in shock as the sky hurtled toward me.

"Rue!" Gabriel grabbed me, enveloping me in the thunderous beat of his wings. I scrambled to get a hold of him, wrapping my legs around his hips and my arms around his neck. "It's okay. It's okay. I have you."

My pulse fluttered in my throat like a frightened moth, making it momentarily impossible to speak, and when I did manage to push out my words, they sounded reedy and strained. "What happened?" I pulled my head from the crook of his shoulder, eyes squinted against the gusts of wind his wings were forcing down on me. "Gabriel?"

Bellows of shock filled the air, and the collective beat of wings surrounded us. I spotted Kabiel with Jilyana in his arms and Asbeel close behind them.

Where were the other three? I twisted in Gabriel's arms, eyes watering as I searched the sky, but movement below drew my attention to Thanatos, where the reason for our abrupt halt and involuntary flight had its jaws wrapped around our godly guide.

The attacker was also a serpent, but larger than Thanatos with spines on its back and a row of black eyes running down its snout. Thanatos whipped back and forth, attempting to be free, but the creature held fast, biting down so that blood welled from the punctures that its teeth had made in the god's armored hide.

The land here was no longer rocky, and a huge hole was visible in the earth several feet from the fight.

Had the thing come out of that? "We have to help him!"

"We can't risk your life," Jilyana said. "We must put the relic first. We can't afford to die here."

The relic *was* our priority, but this god had helped us,

and now he was in danger. "If we walk away now, then we don't deserve to live."

"This isn't our fight," Jilyana said.

"You're right," Gabriel said to her. "So let's make it our fight." He pulled my bat free of the pack Jilyana was holding. "There's a ledge over there where Rue and Jilyana will be safe. What do you say, Kabiel? Fancy taking your newly evolved bodies for a test run?"

Kabiel held up his hand and flicked his wrist so that long black talons erupted from the tips of his fingers. "I thought you'd never ask."

CHAPTER 11

Jilyana and I crouched on a ledge far enough from the battle to be safe but close enough to witness every thrash and slash and hear every scream and bellow.

The watchers and Gabriel took on the spine-ridged serpent with lethal intent, but the bastard was stubborn, refusing to release Thanatos despite the blows raining down on it. It lashed its tail, throwing up clouds of dust which made it difficult to track the fight.

"Asbeel is down!" Jilyana clutched the backpack to her chest, leaning so far forward I was afraid she'd fall off.

"Careful!" I grabbed her shoulder to anchor her, my gaze zipping back to the fight.

The dust cleared long enough for me to catch a glimpse of Asbeel. His bloody face contorted in a snarl as he scrambled to his feet, battle cry lost amidst the chaos as he ran at the attacking serpent.

Where was Gabriel? There, above the spiny serpent's head, swinging my bat at the thing's eyes. Yes! Come on. The other watchers tore at the serpent with their talons, using their spider legs to latch on to it and refusing to be shaken off. I finally saw blood—they'd cut through its thick skin.

It screamed, letting go of Thanatos in the process and swinging its head toward Gabriel. It snapped its blood-coated teeth at the celestial, and my heart shot into my throat, but Gabriel evaded the bite, wings beating hard to take him clear of the threat. Thwarted, the serpent twisted to attack the watchers on its back, but they moved fast to avoid its teeth, raking their way down its body and tearing a fresh scream of pain and rage from it.

It threw back its head, maw wide and yawning as if it wanted to swallow the sky, but in the next moment its body undulated in an arch as it readied to plunge back into the earth.

Shit, the watchers needed to get off it. Now. "Retreat! Retreat now!"

My voice was tiny and insignificant against all the background noise, but they must have realized what was happening because they managed to clear the beast just as it drove into the earth and vanished.

Silence fell, thick and pregnant with foreboding, because although Thanatos was free of his attacker, he lay quiet and unmoving.

"Is he...Is he dead?" Jilyana whispered.

I shook my head as Gabriel flew down to Thanatos and landed by his head. "I don't know...I hope not."

Kabiel joined Gabriel for a few moments, then both he and Asbeel flew toward our ledge.

I scanned Kabiel's face as he drew near. "Is Thanatos okay?"

"I think he's dying. He wants to speak with you. Hurry."

I allowed him to scoop me up and fly me across to the god, leaving Asbeel to bring Jilyana.

Gabriel stood beside Thanatos, his eyes downcast, shoulders slumped.

Kabiel carefully set me on my feet.

"Thanatos?" I hurried over to him. "You wanted to speak to me?"

"I do not have much time here," Thanatos said. "But I need you to understand that your existence is not by chance." A rattling wheeze emanated from his body. "Your god was renowned for always having a plan, even if those plans were never put into motion. I believe you to be one of those plans."

The Cherubim who'd wanted to possess me had explained that I'd been created specially to house a piece of Shem's soul and channel celestial power. I knew this. Which meant I was part of God's plan B to fix things. "Yes, God knew the Morningstar fractured. He sent a Cherubim to find and watch over the pieces. He created me to channel the power. What I don't understand is why he didn't come back and fix things himself."

Thanatos let out a wet chuckle. "Your god has a penchant for creation, but he isn't always present to watch over his worlds. Once the product is done, he becomes distracted. It's the reason why so many of his worlds have destroyed themselves. I suppose we must commend him for putting in place a plan to save yours, even if the success of it rests on a mortal's shoulders." He let out a rattling sigh. "Do not give up, child. This world may seem strange and dangerous to you, but it is home to many creatures, great and small. They deserve to live just as much as your mortals. Even the creatures you call monsters who have found their way into your alien world deserve to live. They did not ask to be displaced. They simply wish to survive, and you can help them all. Restore Lucifer and save us all."

His eyes closed, and a new stillness settled over him.

A permanent kind. "How can he be dead? He said gods were endless."

"I don't know," Kabiel said. "And it hardly matters now."

Gabriel rested his hand on my shoulder. "We should go before any more of those things come out of the ground. Thanatos said those serpents didn't belong in this circle. He said that the fractures were obviously affecting the ecosystem of this world. He warned us not to linger here. To head toward the mountains." Gabriel pointed to the range of shadowy peaks in the distance. "The gateway to the sixth circle is there. He said to pass quickly and not linger."

The ground beneath our feet trembled.

"We take to the air." Kabiel reached for me, but Gabriel hooked his arm around me first.

"I've got her," he said to the watcher. "You can take Jilyana."

Kabiel's silver eyes flashed with annoyance, but he inclined his head and reached for the djinn.

Gabriel's gaze dropped to mine. "It's not a long flight, but it will be easier if you wrap your arms around my neck and your legs about my waist."

Shem had always carried me facing away from him, but he'd had the larger frame of a watcher, and his hands had easily spanned my waist. He'd carried me with my back to his chest, the vibration of his voice rippling up my spine. My eyes heated, and I dropped my gaze.

Dammit. Now wasn't the time to reminisce. "Whatever works." He gripped my hips and lifted me up so I could wrap my legs around him and get into position. His scent filled my head, and I allowed myself to sink into him. He wasn't Shem. No one was Shem. No one would *ever* be

Shem, but it was all right to have this contact with him. It didn't mean anything.

I held tight and closed my eyes. "I'm ready."

He took a breath as if he was about to say something, and I tensed, waiting.

But in the end, it was his wings that spoke, flaring and beating at the air to take us high into a rapidly darkening sky.

My heart sank because in my world when the sun set, shit got bad.

CHAPTER 12

We flew over a long stretch of barren land before a settlement of huts came into view far to our left, behind it forests and a river. These must be home to the Gehennans Thanatos had mentioned. A little farther, and we flew over one of Thanatos's pits, where the souls inside swayed to a tune only they could hear.

What would happen to them now that Thanatos was gone?

Was he truly gone?

He'd said gods were eternal, but what did that mean exactly? If he *was* truly gone, then he was another life lost to our cause. He was another soul that we owed.

We couldn't fail.

I *wouldn't* fail.

My mind whirred, skipping from thought to thought, anything to stop it acknowledging how well my body fit against Gabriel's, how right it felt to be this close to him, and how his bergamot scent made my insides warm.

This attraction was nothing new. We'd spoken of it in the

Golden City, and he'd assured me it was nothing to do with the bond between us—something that would have been out of my control. Which meant I could temper this. Pull back whenever I wanted.

He could bedazzle me, though. Use the bond to make me want him. To render me compliant to his attentions, but I trusted him. Trusted that he wouldn't abuse the connection we'd been forced to forge.

It wasn't him that I had the issue with; it was myself. Because although my mind was against it, my thoughts with Bastian, my emotions tangled in the loss of Shem, my body had other ideas.

I didn't need the complication. It was draining.

Gabriel's grip on me flexed, and he turned his head so that his lips brushed my ear. "It's all right, Rue. You're allowed to relax around me. I would never take advantage."

His warm breath sent a shiver across my nape, and my eyes fluttered closed at the intimacy of the caress. "You said you couldn't read my mind."

"I can't. But the bond allows me to sense your reservations, and it's not a leap to deduce what you're feeling from your body language. You're drawn as tight as the string of a bow." He massaged the small of my back, his large hand spanning it easily, and I bit back a moan.

"Stop that."

He did so immediately. "Relax. I won't bite. Not until you ask me to."

The latter part of the sentence was said with a joking tone, but a shiver of promise skated up my spine regardless. I bit the insides of my cheeks to quell it, my eyes heating in frustration at myself. "That doesn't make me feel any better, Gabriel. All it does is tell me that you *want* to bite me."

His sigh sent another warm breath skating over my skin. “Wanting something and taking it are two separate things.”

But he wanted me, that much was clear. “It’s the bond making you feel things. I thought you said you’d put up shields. Make them stronger.” There was a bite to my tone because I didn’t need this. Not now and probably not ever.

“I have shields active...”

There was a *but* in there somewhere. “What aren’t you telling me?”

“Many things. But now isn’t the time. We’re at the mountains.”

I turned my head to the peaks rushing toward us. Thanatos had been right—we’d been close.

The mountains were a mixture of hardpacked earth and pale blue rock, their summits lost in the churning purple clouds above.

They made a wall that stretched as far as the eye could see, and there didn’t seem to be any way through except over. But the higher we flew, the thinner the air got, and the pinnacles seemed out of reach, almost as if they extended into the stars.

We swooped down and along the barrier, searching for a breach, some way through, but the sun had almost set, and the world was bathed in a soft dusky hue.

It would be night soon, and if we didn’t find a way through these mountains, we’d be stranded here. Out in the open.

Prey for whatever stalked the dark.

Hope was dwindling when Kabiel called out in triumph from ahead of us.

“I see an opening in the mountains!”

We landed smoothly, and Gabriel carefully set me on my feet, his emerald eyes fixed over my head.

I turned to survey the gap Kabiel had spotted. Not a gate but a valley several feet wide, running through the mountain.

"That's not a gate," Jilyana said.

"It must be," Asbeel replied. "Look at these markings on the stone and on the ground." He pointed out the symbols etched into the rocky surface on the mountains at the mouth of the valley. "They're ancient Enochian symbols."

"Can you read them?" Jilyana asked.

"I think so." He ran his fingers over the huge markings. "Before the fall, I spent much of my time in the ancient library with Penemue. We were...friends..."

Why did I get the impression that they'd been more than just friends?

"What does it say?" Gabriel asked.

"It says...Linger and beware the...hidden? I think that says hidden." He frowned. "I'm not sure I've translated that correctly."

Thanatos had warned us not to linger. "It's the beware that bothers me. We should hurry through, then."

Kabiel's gaze dropped to my hand clasped in Gabriel's. When had he taken my hand again? Or had I taken his, and was that disapproval in Kabiel's eyes? Was he wondering how I could possibly be holding hands with someone else so soon after Shem...

No, that was just me.

My shame.

My guilt.

I tugged free of Gabriel's grip and pretended to adjust my jacket. "Kabiel, you can lead. The rest of you flank me and Jilyana."

We passed into the alley in formation, and a gentle prickle of energy washed over me.

"Did you feel that?" Jilyana asked.

My step faltered. "Yes."

"Must have been a ward of some kind," Gabriel said.

The mountains rose on either side of us like a stone cage, not that I was claustrophobic or anything. And as the sky darkened and the stars came out to play, the sense of being trapped retreated.

In fact, it was almost pleasant in the valley. The ground was pebbles and earth, but there were bushes hugging the base of the mountains, each dotted with vibrant flora. The smell, sweet and intoxicating, left me a little lightheaded, but not in a bad way.

Kabiel maintained a lead, his large brown wings flaring and contracting like a pulse while the spider legs remained tucked against his back, the taloned tips a foot off the ground.

He lifted his chin, nostrils flaring slightly as he sniffed the air, and a fist squeezed my heart, because in that moment he reminded me of Shem—feral, ferocious, and wild. I blinked back stupid tears and fixed my attention on the ground, anywhere but on Kabiel.

Something white stuck out of the ground. Kabiel walked past it, but the closer I got, the more certain I was that the thing was a bone.

"Bones," Kabiel confirmed a moment later. "Several piles of them up ahead."

"That's not ominous at all," Gabriel drawled.

We reached the pile of bones, which on closer inspection clearly belonged to two skeletons.

"They look humanoid," Kabiel said, casually picking up a bone. "This creature was maybe four feet tall."

"Gehennans?" Asbeel asked.

"Probably." Kabiel dropped the bone. "Dead Gehennans. Dead for some time."

And they died here? The beware warning at the entrance seemed more potent than ever now, and my gut told me that if we didn't hustle, we might somehow meet the same fate as these Gehennans.

CHAPTER 13

We walked faster after the bone discovery, but the end of the valley still hadn't come into sight.

How long was this path, and why had Thanatos called it a gate?

The sweet fragrance of the blooms spiked for a moment, filling my head with its delightful aroma.

Moonlight looked good on Gabriel. It highlighted his cheekbones and tipped his eyelashes in silver. Fuck, he was beautiful. I shook off the train of thought and fixed my attention on the road ahead.

"What I don't understand is why have a world separated into circles?" Yomiel muttered, his sandy head bowed in thought.

"Why do you care?" Asbeel said. "You have the inanest thoughts sometimes."

"At least I'm able to have thoughts again," Yomiel retorted. "Better than the constant gnawing hunger for flesh."

"I'm afraid it might come back," Kokabel said gruffly. "I

don't want to be a monster again. I don't want to remember the things I've done."

"I can't stop thinking about all the awful things," Matarel said. "And how much I enjoyed doing them at the time."

This watcher's gruff voice was at odds with his lean form which, despite his devolved spiderish form, reminded me more of a bird of prey. He'd kept his thoughts to himself up until now.

They all had.

There was something off about the tone of this conversation. A strange candidness and vulnerability that didn't sit right with the circumstances and situation.

"I see the end of the valley," Gabriel said.

It was still far off, but unmistakably the end of our passage because the blue mountains stopped and a gray expanse began. We must be at the midway point.

We walked faster to eat at the distance between us and the exit, and silence enveloped us for long seconds until Jilyana broke it.

"I was told by my mother that our home world had been separated into domains," she said softly. "Each element had its place, and we did not venture into another elemental's domain without an invitation. Back then, we had our own god, but disaster and war forced us to scatter. Now my people exist in pockets of reality across the multiverse."

Wait, was she saying that the world she wanted to go back to *wasn't* her original world? "Are you saying that our God gave your people refuge?"

"Refuge?" Her lip curled in derision. "I'd hardly call it that. We found an uninhabited world and made it a home. We lived in harmony with nature for decades until your God arrived and claimed that our new world belonged to him. He demanded we leave to make way for his creations. We begged to stay, asserted that we would live in harmony with his creations, but he would not be moved. There was conflict, but our god was gone, and we were no match for yours. We were forced into a hastily created world and trapped there." Her mouth twisted bitterly. "And your god gifted the world we'd vacated to humans."

What the... "You're saying you used to live on earth?"

"It was our home, and then...then it wasn't." Her voice throbbed with sorrow.

The more I learned about God, the more I disliked him. He sounded like an egomaniac on a power trip. "I'm sorry, Jilyana. Sorry for all that you went through."

She offered me a watery smile. "I appreciate that. But the world we were given is home now, and once we fix the Morningstar, I can return to it."

The doorways into her world hadn't been controlled by the Morningstar but by God. I'd have to ask Lucifer if she knew of a way to help Jilyana get home.

In fact, it was time I apologized to the djinn for lying to her. "I wanted to tell you about Lucifer, but I had to be cautious. I had to be sure you weren't going to betray us, and you can't now, so it doesn't matter. And maybe I was a little annoyed with you trying to get Shem back, but that doesn't matter now either. None of it does." What the fuck? Why was I saying all this?

Jilyana stared at me with woe in her eyes, opened her mouth to speak, then pressed it shut again.

"What is happening here?" Kabiel asked.

"I think I know," Kokabel said. "This valley makes you speak truth and tell your secrets. The hidden...it means secrets."

Wait...did that mean the bones belonged to Gehennans that had killed each other?

Jilyana pressed her hand to her mouth and picked up her pace.

We all followed.

The end of the valley was close. We could make it without speaking, right?

But there was a pressure in my throat pushing on my tongue, and words, so many fucking words swirled inside my head.

Kabiel growled softly.

I wanted to ask him if he was okay, but that meant speaking, and I was afraid of what would come out of my mouth. My secrets might not provoke anyone to kill me, but I'd probably want to die of shame afterwards.

Best to keep my mouth shut and the words trapped.

"I wanted to take you the first time I had you pinned to my nest," Kabiel blurted out. His silver eyes brightened with relief then closed on a groan. "Fuck. I still want to fuck you." He slapped himself hard.

My cheeks heated, and Gabriel grabbed my hand, his lips bloodless from how hard he was pressing them together, and for some reason I wanted him to fail. To speak and tell me his deepest, darkest thoughts so that I could reciprocate and tell him how much I hurt. How much Shem's loss had broken me. Broken what could have been, because if Shem had lived then maybe, somewhere down the road, Gabriel and I might have become more than friends. Because it was clear to me now that the attraction between us was more than physical. I found his mind fascinating, and in time, our bond might have flourished, but not now. Not without Shem. Because being with Gabriel would be like cheating on the memory of the watcher that had claimed my heart so wholly it was now a battered, bruised version of itself.

In this moment, I needed to tell Gabriel all of it. Every last word.

Dammit, I needed out of this valley.

I broke into a jog, and the others followed. The exit loomed, the world beyond a gray, dull landscape with the dark canopy of a tree line in the distance.

A ripple of energy passed over my skin. I was out, and the urge to purge my thoughts abated, but my relief was cut short by an icy slap of air that then proceeded to run its hands beneath my clothes.

My gasp of shock froze in my lungs.

"Rue!" Gabriel wrapped his arms around me, and I melted against him, desperate for his heat. "Get back into the valley!" Mist bloomed around my face—my breath and his mingling in the subzero temperatures.

He scooped me up and turned back to the mountain.

"It's blocked off," Kabiel said. "The wards won't let us back in."

"Fuck!" Gabriel hugged me tighter as if he could quell my body's defiant shivering.

My eyeballs hurt from the cold, but I was afraid if I closed my eyes for too long, then they'd stay shut.

"Jilyana, can you summon your fire?" Gabriel asked.

"Not here. I can't. I'm sorry."

"We have to find shelter," Kabiel said. "Build a fire and keep her warm. She won't make it through the night otherwise."

"And what if it doesn't warm up in the morning?" Asbeel asked.

"We'll worry about that when the time comes," Gabriel snapped. "Rue, wrap your body around mine. Do it." He lifted me up, gripping my thighs and urging me to wrap them around his waist.

Part of my rapidly freezing brain wondered if this was going to become our go-to position, but the rest was too busy trying to function.

My limbs were stiff from the cold, but I managed to get into position, tucking my head into the crook of his neck to keep my face warm.

The whoosh of wings flaring cut through the night, and the chill retreated a little.

He'd wrapped his wings around me, bringing them forward over his shoulders to shield me. I didn't know that celestials could use their wings this way, but damn was I grateful for it right now.

"You're okay," Gabriel said. "You'll be okay." His heart beat so fast against me that I doubted his conviction.

The beat of wings told me that some of the watchers had taken to the skies, but my limbs were heavy, and it was getting harder to keep my eyes open.

"I see buildings," Kabiel called out from above. "A settlement not too far from here."

"Lead the way," Gabriel replied, then to me, "Do not fall asleep, Rue. You must stay awake. Hold on to me. That's right, hold tight."

The next moment, we were in motion, his body tight around mine, his arms like bands of steel hugging me to him. How was he running so fast without his arms to balance him? My fingers ached, but that was good. That meant there was still circulation, right?

My eyelids drooped. No. I had to stay awake. Focus on the chill and the pain of it.

Do not fall asleep. But my eyelids fluttered closed anyway.

A low howl rose over the beat of wings, yanking me back to full consciousness.

"Gabriel, what was that?"

"Nothing. It's nothing."

But his racing heart said differently.

Another howl. Then another.

"We have incoming!" Asbeel called.

CHAPTER 14

Danger raked its claws across my scalp as howls lit up the night. "What is it? What's happening?"

"Rue, we must take to the air," Gabriel said. "Hold tight. It won't be for long. I promise."

I pressed myself to his body and squeezed my eyes shut as his wings unfurled from around me. There was no time to adjust to the shock of the icy air shooting over my skin before we rocketed into the sky.

I wanted to look down and see what the threat was, but that meant removing my face from the warmth of Gabriel's neck.

No way was I doing that. "What is it? What's below us?"

"It doesn't matter," Gabriel said. "They won't get us. We're almost at the settlement."

Snarls and growls echoed up into the night.

"They're tracking us," Jilyana called out from somewhere behind us, her voice muffled by the thunder of wingbeats.

Whatever was on the ground couldn't get to us as long as we remained airborne, but the chill up here was heightened, burrowing into my skin and lancing into my bones.

Holding on to Gabriel was no longer an issue. My arms were frozen around his neck, legs locked in place around his waist.

"I see movement in the settlement!" Kabiel called out. "Gehennans, I think. They see us. They have weapons."

"We have to land," Gabriel said. "It's the settlement or the wilds."

We dropped altitude, and my head swam with the need to pass out. I clung to consciousness, battling the darkness that threatened to consume me. The impact of landing jolted me awake.

Voices yelled at us, babbling in a language I didn't understand.

Gabriel wrapped his wings around me once more, and warmth ate away at the chill that had me in its grip.

"They can't get in," Jilyana said. "That must be some kind of barrier."

My mouth moved against Gabriel's skin as I spoke "What...what's happening?"

"Asbeel is speaking to the Gehennans. I think he's getting through to them. The beasts tracking us are gone. They turned away once we hit the settlement. I think there's a ward or some kind of barrier around this place to keep them at bay." He stroked my back, his hand leaving a trail of heat up my spine. "Are you all right? Warmer now?"

"I'm so sleepy."

"We need to get some food in you."

"This way," Asbeel said. "They're extending hospitality and will show us the way to the bridge tomorrow."

"I want to see." I tried to lift my head, but it felt like a boulder on my shoulders.

"Later," Gabriel said. "We need to warm you up and feed you first."

I allowed him to take the lead and carry me to wherever we'd be bunking for the night.

Someone babbled in a low melodious voice, and Asbeel responded in a similar tone.

"They're letting us have their barn for the night," Asbeel said. "It's the only building that will accommodate our sizes."

The creak of a door followed, and Gabriel ducked his head, curling his body around mine to fit through the frame and into a building.

"It's warmer in here," Jilyana said.

Gabriel freed me from the cocoon of his wings, and I got my first look at our temporary shelter. The barn was small, the floor covered in sawdust, but there was a second level in the rafters and bales of hay to make a bed with. The air was cold but not icy. Jilyana was right; it *was* warmer—still cold, but not deathly so.

"We can't build a fire in here," Asbeel said. "They say it's not permitted, but he's gone to fetch us some blankets. Not that we need them, but the females might."

Jilyana smiled up at him. "I'm fine. I don't feel the cold."

"I'll take them all." My voice sounded small. Fuck, I was tired.

"Can we get some hot food?" Gabriel asked Asbeel.

The watcher nodded. "I'll see what I can do." He ducked out of the building, letting in a gust of bone-chilling air in the process.

I pressed closer to Gabriel, and he rubbed my back again, his huge hand sweeping up and down to warm me.

"Let's get you settled," he said. "We'll take the rafters. Heat rises." He flew us up to the balcony, which was littered with crates and a few sacks. I was still pressed to his chest, my legs locked around him.

He gently grasped my thighs. "How stiff are you? Can you—"

"Yes. I can." I peeled myself off him, legs folding under me as soon as my boots hit the rafters. "I'm good. I'm just going to...to sit here."

His jaw ticked, and he looked as if he wanted to argue, but then he gave me a curt nod and set to work moving boxes and arranging sacks to make a snug sleeping area.

I didn't protest as he scooped me up and carried me to my makeshift bed. Lying down sounded like bliss even if the sack was rough and smelled funky. A shiver ran over me, and my teeth began to chatter.

Gabriel pressed his palm to my cheek, then my neck. "You're as cold as ice."

"I feel like shit."

"Gabriel?" Asbeel appeared by the balcony nursing a mug of something. "They have broth, or something that resembles it."

Gabriel brought the mug over to me. "Try this."

"What if it's poisonous to me?"

"Shit. I hadn't considered that." He set it down. "Bastian packed supplies?"

I managed a nod. "Jilyana has them."

He brushed a tendril of hair off my cheek, his emerald gaze dark with concern. "I'll be right back."

It was as if his absence made the chill inside me stronger, forcing me to curl up for warmth.

"Rue? Here, eat this. Rue?" Gabriel patted my cheek.

I forced my eyes open. "Too tired."

His jaw tensed. "Rue, do you trust me?"

"Yes."

"Good, because what I'm going to suggest might sound unseemly, but I think it will help immensely."

"What is it?"

"Body heat," he said. "Skin-on-skin contact."

Heat sounded good. "Okay."

He blinked sharply. "You'll have to be naked. We both will. You understand that?"

He really didn't know me yet. "You want to get naked and cuddle so I can stop feeling like I have ice in my veins."

"Yes."

"I'm good with that."

The corner of his mouth lifted slightly. "You never fail to surprise me."

"And you're taking too long to strip and share your heat."

He put a blanket over me, too light to help stave off the chill much. "Take off your clothes."

But my fingers were clumsy, still tingly and numb from the chill. "Help me."

His throat bobbed, but he nodded. "Let me just..." He shrugged off his shirt and pushed down his pants so that he was naked except for his underwear. Part of my mind registered the hard flat planes of his chest and torso, lines curving and meeting to create perfection, but it was difficult to enjoy the view when my teeth were chattering.

He climbed onto the makeshift bed behind me and got under the blanket. His body heat beat at my clothes, promising blessed relief that galvanized me into action. I fumbled with my shirt, desperate to pull my arms free, but stuck. "Urgh."

"Slow down." Gabriel extricated me, then pulled the shirt over my head. I shuffled back against him until my back met his chest and sighed when his body heat kissed my skin.

"That feels so fucking good."

"It will feel better if you take your trousers off. May I?"

"Yes, please."

His hot fingers grazed my cold skin, then slipped beneath my waistband for a moment as he gained purchase enough to draw my pants down over my hips, leaving my underwear in place. The trail of warmth he left tore another sigh of pleasure from me.

"Maybe don't make such sounds," he said in a low voice. "I'm a celestial, not a saint."

He splayed his palm across my abdomen, and the pulse between my thighs throbbed, wanting more because this felt good. This felt right, but it wasn't. It couldn't be.

I licked my lips. "Just body heat, Gabriel."

"I know." He pulled me closer, spooning me and feeding me the nectar I needed.

My muscles relaxed, and my eyes drifted closed.

"Sleep now, Rue. I've got you."

I was afraid of just that.

CHAPTER 15

MICHAEL

With title of Supracelestia comes new hungers. The guilt of my past has been lifted by the power that courses through me, and this body... This wonderous body must be fed.

The human I've chosen to pleasure me has long, dark hair and large gray eyes. Her body is soft and supple, not as toned as I'd like. Not as athletic, but it will do. Yes, it will do.

She stares up at me in awe and wonder, her mouth parted in ecstasy as I fill her again and again, each thrust deeper, harder, until she's crying out incoherently.

I cover her face with my palm, focusing on her body, on her breasts as they bounce with every penetration.

"Yes, Michael, yes. I want you." Her voice is breathless and wanton. "It's always been you."

"Yes, Rue, you want this. You've always wanted it. I saw how you looked at me. The way you touched me. But you were afraid of him, of what he'd say or do. But he's gone now. He's gone, and you can be mine."

"Yes, I want you. It's always been you," she repeats.

Light swells between us, but I pull it back into myself, body shuddering with a release that is all too mortal. A pleasure I've missed.

The woman's thighs quiver with her own release, hot wetness blooming between us as she proves how much she's enjoyed our interaction.

But she has no idea how close she's come to being obliterated by my light. Only a bonded female can withstand the light of celestial procreation.

She moans softly. "Did I do good?"

"Yes. Yes, you did." I slide my hand down her face to her collarbones and then lower, trailing my fingers down her abdomen.

How was this wonder left in the mixer for so long? I'm glad I claimed her before they could mark her as a Potential.

I might make her mine. Now that my connection to Bee is dead, I'm free to form another.

I smooth her hair back from her face. A face, that on prolonged consideration, looks less and less like Rue.

She whimpers softly in protest as I pull out of her.

"Please...more." She grabs at my wrists.

My aura is strong, my power unmatched, and this female is bedazzled by it even though we are not bonded.

She rolls her hips. "Please."

I click my fingers, and she falls back onto the bed, asleep. Like this, in this light, at that angle, she does look like Rue. I might keep her. For now. But once the Dominion's plan is complete and I have the leave to do so, I will find Rue. I will find her, and I will bring her home.

Until then...I run my hand up the woman's flank, and

she shivers beneath my touch. "Yes, until then this will do just fine."

There's a knock at the main doors to my quarters. I close the bedchamber and cross the polished wooden floor to answer it.

A sentinel stands outside looking nervous. I remember this look. The awe, the fear. How I've missed it. "What?"

"Supracelestia, the scout team has sent a message that they have found a church which was not there previously, and within the church there is a conjunction."

"What do you mean the church wasn't there previously?"

"The sentinels who have flown over the area many times have said that it was never visible before."

A church hidden from celestial eyes until now...It had to be sitting on a crossing, which would explain the conjunction and the ward around it that rendered it invisible to certain eyes... "Go on..."

"There is evidence that humans may have been living there, but they are gone now. We believe that they found the conjunction. We believe it leads to Gehenna."

"You think the humans went through?"

"If they did, then they will be dead."

"Then check. Send a party through." I don't bother to mask my irritation.

"They are unable to pass. The conjunction is locked to them."

"Is that all?"

He inclines his head. "They await your instructions."

I'm tempted to ignore the Dominion's orders and go after them. To scout the surrounding area for the humans. If I thought Rue might be among them, I might, but if there is a conjunction in the church, then my bet is that Rue has gone through it, which means she's discovered more about Gehenna than she should.

"Tell them to set a watch on the conjunction and to alert me if anyone comes through. I'll brief the Dominion."

He inclines his head, backing up a few steps before turning on his heel and hurrying away.

I head back to the bedchamber and don my armor. I should wake the woman and send her back to the nest with all the other human females yet unclaimed, but I doubt I'll be with the Dominion for long, and the nights can be lonely. She's safer here with me than in the mixer or in the nest. Not all the celestials are as gentle as I am.

I close the door softly and leave her to her slumber. I have business to attend to. Playtime will have to wait.

CHAPTER 16

BEE

Frightened, tired faces fill the old service station that we've chosen for the night. Everyone is exhausted from the long day on the road, but there is hope too. We're one day down, no attacks or casualties, and we have a roof over our heads.

The reapers and watchers have organized an internal patrol while the devolved patrol outside.

We're as safe as we can be, for now.

While Mira gets everyone settled and fed, I join Bastian at the back of the building in a small storeroom, where he's going through some boxes left over by the previous occupants, looking for supplies.

"Anything?"

"Nothing worth getting excited about." He shoves a box away from him with an exasperated sigh which I'm certain has nothing to do with the lack of viable goods in the boxes, and his next words confirm my suspicion. "I can't stop wondering if she's okay. The monsters come from that place, and she's gone there."

I've been thinking the same thing. All I can do to console him is repeat the words I've been saying to myself ever since we left the church. "She has watchers with her. Gabriel too. They'll protect her. I mean, can you see anything getting past them?"

He pinches the bridge of his nose. "I just...I should be with her."

"No, you shouldn't. You just want to, and I get that. I wish I could be with her too. Being here...making this journey, important as it is, feels like being on hold."

His gaze darts up to meet mine. "That's exactly it. I feel like we're on pause. Waiting."

"We have a purpose too. Once we get to this base, you can see what's on the flash drive..."

"Yes." His jaw hardens. "Find out what the fucking Dominion is hiding."

This, sorting through boxes is a distraction. A way to keep his mind from dwelling on the woman he loves. I don't blame him. Our Rue walked into the belly of the beast, and we can do nothing but wait to see if she's devoured or manages to cut her way out.

I grab a box. "We'll get through these faster if we work together."

He offers me a small smile that says he knows exactly what I'm doing but doesn't call me out.

We get to work in companionable silence, and for a little while, the world feels like less of a fucked-up place.

An hour passes quickly, and we're on the last storage unit of boxes when I notice a seam in the wall behind the unit. "Bastian, I think there's a door back here."

He stops what he's doing to join me, peering into the gloom behind the shelves. "You're right. I think there is."

My curiosity is piqued, and I can see that his is too.

What's behind the door? Why is it sealed? "Monsters?"

"This unit doesn't look like it's been moved for...well, years." He swipes at the thick layer of dust and grime, then points at the rusted bolts that hold it to the wall. "Well before the monsters came."

"Then, what?"

His eyes fill with the light of mischief. "Should we?"

"It might not be monsters, but it could still be dangerous. Why hide it otherwise?"

He arches a brow. "Valuable?"

"Money and jewels hardly matter in our world."

"True, but...wouldn't it be nice to know?"

I can't lie. I'm intrigued. "Fine. But we should have backup before we—"

"Wait here." He hurries off but is back a few minutes later with Erelim, Tumiel, and Sarq. "Now we have backup."

It takes fifteen minutes to get the unit off the wall and expose the hidden door. The door is locked and bolted, but neither measure is any match for the watchers. The door pops open, and musty air spills out.

We back up as Erelim takes the lead, his scythe glowing to light up the room beyond. It illuminates a short set of stone steps and a stone floor and the back of something large and metallic.

Erelim descends the short flight and holds out his scythe to illuminate the back of a large vehicle, studded with metallic spikes. "What the—"

There's a whirr, and then the lights come on, illuminating the whole room, which is filled with crates. In the middle of it sit two repurposed minibuses. Huge off-road wheels, viscous bumpers, and spikes all over their body.

"Fuck..." Bastian steps forward. "Someone was preparing. Someone knew what was coming."

Tumiel cracks open a crate. "Non-perishables," he says.

Supplies...This whole room is filled with supplies.

Bastian finds his way under the hood of the nearest bus. "Built to take a variety of fuel. This baby is perfect."

"Keys?" Tumiel asks.

Bastian yanks on the door, his expression tight, as if he's afraid it'll be locked and we'll have to smash a window, but it opens with a pop. He dives in, and long seconds pass before he calls out, "Found them. Under the seat."

He emerges, keys in hand, a huge grin on his face, and the mood feels immediately lighter.

"Someone planned but never got to execute it," Tumiel says.

"How could they have known?" Bastian asks. "There was no warning. Nothing."

"There are those who can see," Erelim says. "Prophets, blessed with a direct line to God. In the old days, when man was new, people revered the prophets. But as man evolved, as society moved toward technology, science became the new god, and the connection between a prophet and the heavens grew weaker."

"If that's the case, if whoever did this was a prophet, it means that God knew what was about to happen, and instead of stopping it, he sent a message to some man or woman knowing full well that no one would fucking believe them."

"What happened to the prophet, do you think?" Tumiel asks in a small voice. "After all their preparation..."

He or she was obviously dead. This place, locked up tight and abandoned, was proof of that.

"Their efforts won't go to waste," Bastian says. "We'll load up with as many supplies as we can and drive ourselves to base zero. Better to come bearing gifts, right?"

The use of the vehicles would take a day off our journey. Now all we had to hope was that the occupants of base zero honored their connection to Gabriel and let us in.

CHAPTER 17

GABRIEL

Rue's body is warm now, working effectively to keep her that way. I'm tempted to stay with her just to keep holding her. She's soft and pliant in my arms, so fragile in sleep, yet so strong-willed in nature. I find myself wanting to know more. To understand her more. Just...more. But her grief is like a beacon that holds me at bay. Now is not the time to make my feelings known. They do not matter. All that matters is her, and now that she's safe, I have work to do.

I leave her tucked beneath the blanket, dress, and join the others on the floor below.

Jilyana is asleep, curled on a sack beneath the balcony. Do djinn need to sleep, or is she playacting? Not that it matters now that Rue's spilled the secret about Lucifer. I'm sure Jilyana will confront her about it in due course; it would be telling if she didn't. I'll be able to gauge her trustworthiness based on that conversation, but for now, we need to plan for the dawn.

The watchers are huddled in a circle talking in low voices. Kabiel looks up as I approach.

"I assume she's recovering, or you wouldn't be down here," he says, his tone almost accusatory.

"You assume correctly. We need to discuss our plan for tomorrow. Asbeel, can you find out what the temperatures are like in this circle during the day?"

"I already have. It'll be cold but not subzero. They've offered to provide us with furs for our journey. The bridge is several miles away from here, but they've agreed to send a guide with us. The creatures that chased us won't be a threat going forward; Xelion said they only inhabit the territory close to the valley we came out of."

"But they don't attack the settlement?"

"No, the Gehennans have an agreement with the pack. They're a peaceful people, but they did warn that the Gehennans in the fifth circle are not so peaceful."

I barely remember details about our hosts except their small size and the fact that their bodies are covered in thick fur. Rue was my focus at the time.

"We'll leave at dawn," Asbeel says. "We should reach the bridge by midday."

"What about the guardian that Thanatos mentioned?" Kokabel asks.

"The leader of the settlement said that midday is a good time to cross. The guardian is usually absent."

"Strange to put a guardian on a bridge and not have him guard it at all times," Matarel says. "If this Zeus wants to stop Gehennans leaving the circle, surely she should have a guardian who is forever present."

"Does it matter?" Yomiel says. "As long as we get over the bridge."

"Do you truly think my thoughts are inane?" Yomiel asks Kokabel suddenly.

Kokabel snorts. "That isn't much of a secret."

Secrets...Yes, much was said in the valley. All kinds of minor confessions were made. My gaze drifts to Kabiel to find him looking right at me, his chin hard, his pale eyes defiant.

"We need to talk. Outside."

He nods. "I suppose we do."

A COUPLE of Gehennans are stationed outside the barn holding spears. They look up at me with huge dark eyes that beg me not to do anything stupid. They say they're a peaceful people, but I'd wager that peace came at a cost, and I'm certain they have the ability to protect it with violence if need be.

I hold up both hands in what I hope is a universal gesture of peace, and they back away to give me room to stretch my wings. The awe on their faces makes me wonder if they've ever seen a celestial before or any winged being, for that matter. Are there any birds in this circle? In this world even?

"Go on, then," Kabiel says as he joins me outside. "Warn me to stay away from her."

Kabiel and I never moved in the same circles in heaven, so he has no idea how I think. "Why would I do that?"

He frowns down at me. "Why would you not?"

"Because I don't see you as a threat. I see you as a protector." I give him a moment to absorb this before continuing. "Rue is special, and she'll remain that way, even after we hand over the relic pieces to Lucifer. She's a channel to the Morningstar power, to Lucifer's power, and Lucifer is aware of that fact."

His eyes narrow. "You think Lucifer will try to hurt Rue?"

Good. He catches on fast. "I don't know. I'm not sure of anything right now except that we must do whatever it takes to keep Rue safe."

"And you trust me to do that." He snorts softly, the sound self-deprecating. "Shem would disagree."

"Why would you think that?"

"He called me a monster."

"And were you acting like one at the time?"

He falls silent, and I have my answer. "You could have taken Rue by force the first time you had her in your nest—a time when you were devolved, a monster, as you like to call yourself—and yet you did not. Even back then, you had enough control, enough of a grasp on your hunger, to make the right choice, and now...Now that you've developed feelings for Rue, I know for certain that you won't harm her."

He goes as still as stone. "How can you know that?"

"What? That you have feelings for her or that you won't harm her?"

"Both."

"I was trained to see things, Kabiel. To read body language and tone of voice. To know. And I know you're falling for her."

He's silent for several beats, processing. I like that he thinks before he speaks. It means we'll get on.

"She doesn't reciprocate," he says finally.

No. No she doesn't. "But does that matter?"

This time, there's no hesitation. "No. It doesn't matter. Does it matter to you that she reciprocates but will never act on her feelings toward you?"

His words tease the hollow space inside me that this knowledge has created. "You have the gift of insight, too, it seems."

He chuckles wryly. "You didn't answer my question."

Ah, he's persistent too. I like that, and so I answer. "I chose to protect Rue even before Shem made me vow to do so. Yes, my feelings for her are growing into...more, but I will never press them on her. Once this world is safe, I'll leave. Putting distance between us will hopefully mute the bond."

"It's getting stronger, isn't it?"

"Yes. Yes it is. But I can control it. I know I can. I will not take what is not freely given."

"And if you can't control it?"

"Then you'll stop me from consummating it."

He turns to look me in the eye, his expression almost pitying. "Yes. Yes, I will."

And that will have to be enough.

CHAPTER 18

RUE

"It's warm and cozy here with you." I snuggled against Shem, and he stroked my hair. "Can't we just stay in bed all day?"

"We have a world to save." He kissed the top of my head. "But I'd like nothing better than to stay here with you. Forever."

I closed my eyes and reveled in the moment. These moments of bliss in a world that had fallen into chaos were few and far between. They were tiny treasures to be memorized and savored every time shit hit the fan.

"Rue, you need to wake up and eat something."

"I thought we were staying in bed to snuggle?"

He shook me.

"Shem, stop it."

The hand on my shoulder stilled, and the warm, fuzzy feeling evaporated as the dream slipped away.

"Are you awake now?" Gabriel asked gently.

I was awake, but I needed a moment to battle the crushing weight of despair that had settled on my chest.

Gabriel sighed. "I'm sorry to pull you from your dreams, but you need to eat."

I sat up, clutching the blanket to my chest. "Thank you."

He opened a protein bar and held it out, but the thought of food made my stomach queasy. Hunger was a thing of the past, and even though I knew my body needed food, I didn't crave it.

He broke off a piece and held it up to my lips. "Please."

My stupid eyes heated as I accepted the offering. He fed me the rest, piece by piece, in silence, then handed me a bottle of water.

"It will get easier with time. I can promise you that," he said.

"I don't know if I want it to get easier. I don't want to forget."

"You won't forget, Rue. But the memories you have won't cause you so much pain."

Pain...the dream had left me in pain. Left me with an aching void inside that felt like it would never be filled. Shem had taken a part of me into oblivion with him, and I would never be whole again.

"Get some sleep," Gabriel said.

"I don't want to dream."

He pressed his lips together. "I can lie with you if you like. We can talk."

I forced my lips into a smile that echoed my gratitude. "I'd like that."

He handed me my clothes. "You might want to put these on first."

He turned away while I dressed. "I'm done."

We settled under the blanket together, face to face this

time because spooning was much too intimate when I wasn't freezing to death.

"How long till dawn, do you think?"

"I'm not sure," he said. "Several hours...The locals have agreed to escort us to the bridge. They'll also provide us with some furs for you and Jilyana."

Jilyana...Shit. "She knows about Lucifer now."

His expression was serious. "Yes, so be on your guard."

He still didn't trust her. "I know she did some bad shit, believe me I know, but she's trying to atone."

"That's her story, and if it's true, then we have lost nothing, but if she's lying and we're not on our guard, then we risk losing everything."

"Even if she did want the relics, now she knows we're taking them to Lucifer, her plan is fucked. She won't get a chance to steal them off us when we get out of here because we'll no longer have them." But I didn't believe that. I didn't believe Jilyana would betray us. Betraying us would negate everything Shem stood for. It would be a slap in the face to his sacrifice.

"Will you promise me something?" Gabriel asked.

"What?"

"You won't hand over those relics until I've spoken to Lucifer."

"Why?"

"I just need to gauge her true intentions."

"You think she lied? That she can't fix things?"

"I'm concerned what will happen to you once Lucifer is whole and in control of her power again. What she will do to a mortal able to channel the power that belongs to her."

My pulse skipped. "I...I didn't think about that."

"That's why you have me, Rue. I'll always consider every angle."

"Do you think she'll kill me? No. Don't answer that. It doesn't matter. As long as she saves my world, I don't care what happens to me. Shem isn't the only one who can make a sacrifice."

"And what about Bastian? You think he'd be happy hearing you speak like this?"

He didn't know Bastian at all. "Bastian would do the same thing if it meant saving humanity."

His mouth tightened at the corners. "Well, I won't allow it to come to that."

"What?" I smiled up at him playfully. "You'll fight Lucifer? God's favorite?"

His gaze bore into me with intensity. "Yes, Rue. I will fight to keep you safe. Always."

My pulse sped up, and the urge to press closer to him washed over me. "This bond thing is powerful, isn't it?" I was aiming for a light, teasing tone but delivered an intimate whisper instead.

Gabriel slid his hand into my hair, angling my head so our mouths were inches apart. "This isn't just the bond, Rue, but if it's easier for you to believe that, then so be it."

I wanted him to kiss me, but I needed him to stop touching me. I wanted him to pull me into his arms, but I needed space from him.

He slowly pulled away. Had he sensed the tumult of emotions bubbling inside me?

"This bond isn't going anywhere, Rue, but I swear to you that I won't let it ruin our friendship."

Friendship. Yes. We were friends. I needed that. "Thank you."

"Now close your eyes. Rest."

I didn't want to dream of Shem, not while I was lying with Gabriel, but my eyelids were heavy, and I needed to recharge before the rest of our journey. So I tucked my arms against my chest, dropped my forehead to his collarbone, and closed my eyes. After a few moments, he put his arm around me, and when I didn't protest, he relaxed. A few weeks ago, if someone had described Gabriel as sweet, I'd have laughed in their face. Gabriel was a strategist, a warrior, a rebel, but he was also considerate, empathic, kind, and...sweet. Yes. Gabriel was sweet, and with all the bitterness in my life right now, I could do with a little sweet.

I'd take what I could get and hope that it didn't become an addiction.

That *he* didn't become an addiction.

CHAPTER 19

The sun was rising by the time Gabriel flew us down from the rafters to join the others on the ground floor of the barn.

"The settlement leader had furs sent over." Kabiel handed me a bundle. "Put them on."

Jilyana was already dressed in hers, but she busied herself with adjusting them when I looked over, dodging my gaze.

I couldn't avoid this conversation, no matter how much I might want to. "Jilyana, we need to talk."

She shook her head. "I know what you want to talk about, but it's fine. We don't have to. I understand your reservations."

She was giving me an out, but I didn't want an out. "Look. I like you, and I want to trust you, but I don't have the luxury of putting my wants above the safety of everyone else. So I decided not to tell you the whole truth about our trip."

"I understand." Her smile was weak. "I knew atonement

would be hard. I'm determined to prove myself. But if you'd rather someone else keep hold of the relics, then—"

"No. You can keep hold of them. For now."

Her throat bobbed as she slung the pack onto her shoulder. "Thank you."

The door to the barn opened, and I got my first look at a Gehennan. Humanoid, four feet tall, and covered in fur, the creature had no need for clothes, but he was wearing boots and had a pack on his back. His heart-shaped face was the only hairless part. I kept thinking he—I mean, was he a male? It was impossible to tell as the hair covered everything, and females might not have breasts in this world.

The Gehennan scanned our party with large brown eyes and zeroed in on Asbeel before speaking in his native tongue.

Asbeel listened, then responded in a stilted way before addressing us. "He says that they're ready to lead us, but they can't go farther than the angry skies. At least, that's what I think he said. He warns us not to fly through the angry skies. He said we'll have to go on foot through that area."

"What does that mean?" Gabriel asked. "Angry skies? A storm?"

"Most probably."

"We've flown through worse," Kokabel said. "Tell him he need not worry."

Asbeel relayed that, and the Gehennan snorted and lifted his chin as if to say *whatever*.

"Why are they being so helpful?" Jilyana asked abruptly. "Did you tell them why we're here and what's happening?"

"Yes," Asbeel said. "They had no trouble believing me. They're very in tune with the ecosystem of their circle and have noticed changes the past few years. They've never traveled out of the sixth circle but have heard tales of the inner circles and their queen."

The Gehennan said something, and Asbeel nodded.

"He says we need to leave now."

We followed him out into the gray dawn, into the chill that was made bearable by the lightweight yet warm furs they'd provided.

Two more Gehennans waited, each carrying spears, and behind them was a cart attached to two animals that looked like a cross between a pony and a hound. Mist plumed from their nostrils as they pawed at the ground, eager to be on their way.

Gabriel held his arms out to me, but Kabiel stepped forward.

"I'll carry Rue this time," he said. "If that's all right with Rue."

He'd confessed to wanting to fuck me. I should be disgusted, but I wasn't. Kabiel fought his devolution at every step. He fought every dark urge, every debased thought, and there was nobility in that. There was honor and strength in it. How could I be disgusted by that? It wasn't fair to press temptation on him by accepting his offer, but turning it down would be like a slap.

He might think that I *was* disgusted by him. I didn't want that, so I looked to Gabriel, expecting him to protest and save me from the conundrum, but Gabriel simply shrugged as if he didn't care.

He didn't want to fly me?

Why did I care? I didn't. "That's fine, Kabiel. Thanks."

Kabiel blinked sharply. He'd obviously expected me to put up a fight.

"Jilyana, I can carry you," Asbeel said to the djinn.

Jilyana's eyes lit up for a moment but then dimmed. "Thank you." She adjusted the pack so that it hung in front of her, the handle of my bat poking out of one side.

Kabiel had the same build as Shem, so he'd be able to carry me like Shem had, and it would be less intimate, thank goodness. I stood with my back to him, and he wrapped his arms around my torso.

"You ready?"

"Yes."

We took to the air, and below us, the cart rattled into motion.

"About what I said in the valley...I'm sorry if I offended you."

"Offended me by telling me I was fuckable? Hardly."

He let out a surprised laugh. "You're not disgusted by me?"

"Admittedly, I'm not a fan of spiders, but you're more than your devolved form, Kabiel. I'm not disgusted. I'm not afraid, and truth be told, I trust you. I know that you'll never willingly hurt me."

He was silent for several seconds, the only sound the beat of his wings and the whoosh of air around us. When he finally spoke, his tone was thick with emotion.

"Thank you."

The rest of the journey passed in companiable silence. Whereas the seventh circle had been all but barren, the sixth was a lush landscape of forests and green grasses. I spotted a settlement in the distance—a sprawling area of small buildings with farmland beyond—and to our left was a field of yellow and red flowers swaying in the breeze. These hardy blooms didn't seem to mind the chill.

The skies might be gray, but the world seemed filled

with sunshine, until it wasn't. At least not in the distance where the sky churned with dark clouds.

The Gehennans called out to us and drew their cart to a halt.

Asbeel, who was flying ahead of us, swooped down with Jilyana and landed beside the cart.

"It looks like we may have reached the angry skies," Kabiel said, easing into a hover, wings beating periodically to keep us airborne. Gabriel and the other watchers joined us above the cart trail a moment later.

Asbeel finished speaking to the civilians, then joined us with Jilyana. "They're turning back. They said to follow the trail and we'll come to a road. They called it the glass road, if I'm understanding correctly. We must stay on it. They suggested to go on foot."

"On foot will take longer," Kokabel said. "I say we stay airborne for as long as possible."

"Agreed," Kabiel said.

"They must have a reason for warning against it," Matarel said.

"I agree with Matarel," Gabriel said. "But I also agree we should remain airborne until we know more about these angry skies."

As the Gehennans' cart retreated, we flew on, staying above the trail, closer and closer to a sky that looked as if it was raging with dark emotions. The temperature dropped, and a strange crackle filled the air, along with the scent of a storm.

"It's getting windy!" Gabriel called out.

"We can manage," Kokabel called out, picking up speed toward the forbidden elements ahead.

Kabiel's grip on me tightened as we also sped up.

Gabriel and Asbeel flanked us with Matarel and Yomiel close behind.

The air was thicker beneath the angry sky, charged with energy that pricked at my skin. The trail below died and was replaced by an area of black, glassy-looking land. It was a wide strip with jagged edges where the earth sparkled like diamonds, and beyond it was nothing but sand.

"It's a beach," Kabiel said. "A beach that has been turned to glass."

I knew enough about the elements, enough science to know that this phenomenon only happened if—

A roar battered my eardrums, shattering my thoughts, and then dazzling fingers of lightning cut across our path.

Asbeel swerved to avoid being hit.

"Down! Get down!" Gabriel cried.

Another crack. Another blaze of light.

"Watch out!" Gabriel slammed into us, shoving us out of the path of a strike and taking it himself.

His body lit up as the lightning energy held him suspended in the air for what felt like an eternity but couldn't have been more than a few moments, then he was falling, and all I could do was scream.

CHAPTER 20

"Gabriel!" My scream was eclipsed by another crack of thunder. Gabriel hit the ground and didn't get back up. "Gabriel!"

My throat hurt, my ears rang, and adrenaline burned a path through my veins as Kabiel continued to fly past Gabriel. Away from Gabriel. "Stop! We have to get him. We have to go back."

"No. I need to get you to safety."

Gabriel was hurt. He was fucking hurt and Kabiel wasn't fucking stopping. I thrashed in his arms, trying to twist my body, trying to look back, trying to break free, but Kabiel held me tighter, swerving and diving to avoid the streaks of lightning that cut zigzag paths in front of us. The hiss and crack in the air, so loud it smothered my screams, should have terrified me, but there was no room for terror with rage flooding my veins.

"Take me back! Take me back, you bastard!"

I was so focused on my ire that I didn't notice that we were out from beneath the angry sky until Kabiel began to descend.

We hit the ground, and he set me on my feet but didn't let go. "Calm down."

My breath came hard and fast. Calm was far out of reach. "You left him. You fucking left him! We have to go back! Now!"

"No need." Kabiel turned me to face the glass road and the angry sky that ended several feet away from us.

Asbeel landed with Jilyana a moment later, but my gaze zeroed in on Yomiel running toward us with Gabriel slung over his shoulder. Kokabel and Matarel were close behind.

A sob of relief tore from my throat.

"You really thought we'd leave him?" Kabiel asked.

I glanced up at him in time to catch the disappointment in his eyes, but I didn't have time to soothe his ego.

Gabriel was hurt. I broke away from him and ran toward Yomiel.

He carefully set Gabriel on the ground.

"Gabriel?" I crouched beside him. "Hey." My fingers trembled as I reached out to touch his cheek. Cold...so cold...

His eyes were closed, chest rising and falling rapidly in a way that told me he was in shock, unsurprising considering the state of his torso—a charred, blackened mess where the lightning had struck him.

"The damage is extensive," Yomiel said. "He's not healing."

It was okay. It would be okay. "I can help. I can heal him."

"Morningstar power doesn't work on celestials like it does on watchers, Rue," Kabiel said softly.

A vise gripped my lungs. "I can try. I have to try."

Gabriel cracked open one eye, but it wasn't me he looked at; it was Kabiel. "Protect...her."

"I will. I swear it," Kabiel said.

Like hell were we doing this. I gripped Gabriel's chin and forced him to look at me. "You are *not* going to die. I won't let you. Where's the serum?" He must have brought some serum. I patted his pockets, but they were empty. "Where is it?" His eyes rolled, and a sob bubbled up my throat, but I swallowed it. There was time. There had to be time. "Where's the fucking serum?"

"Didn't bring any." His eyes fluttered closed.

"It wouldn't have been enough," Kabiel said. "He'll need a huge injection of celestial energy to heal him. More than a vial could give. More than ten could give."

He was saying it was futile, but I didn't accept that. I wouldn't. I'd failed to save Shem, and I'd be damned if I lost Gabriel too.

I slapped his cheek. "Wake up. You have to stay awake." I couldn't lose another person I cared about. "You need to heal." But he was heavy and limp in my arms, his breath shallow and reedy. My vision blurred. "Please, Gabriel... don't you...don't you dare..." I blinked back tears and gripped him harder, my eyes blazing with enough determination for the both of us. "Wake the fuck up!"

Kabiel touched my shoulders lightly. "Rue, I don't think—"

Panic flooded my senses. "No."

I pressed my palm to Gabriel's charred chest, and the fact he didn't cry out in pain told me how severe these injuries were, so bad that the sensory vessels in his body were dead. The scout in me said this was good, that he would die painlessly now, but right now, I wasn't a scout. I was a woman determined to save someone precious, so I shut the voice down. He was not dying today.

I opened the channel to the Morningstar power,

allowing it to rush through me and into Gabriel.

The tugging sensation at my solar plexus intensified.

I was losing him.

This wasn't working.

But then a low-grade vibration filled me, and his charred skin began to knit and recover.

"It's working," Asbeel said in a hushed tone. "How is it working?"

"The bond…" Kabiel said. "I think this must have something to do with the bond they share."

I continued to channel until his skin was smooth and unmarred. "Gabriel? Wake up. You're okay. I fixed you. You're okay now." But even as I said it, I knew it to be a lie. The special connection between us that had become so much a part of me the past few weeks that I barely noticed it was gone.

"He's gone," Yomiel confirmed flatly.

A strange calm settled over me—an eerie emptiness that part of me recognized as the absence of him.

He'd been with me all this time.

His essence, connected to mine through the bond.

He'd been there, silent and unintrusive but exuding security. But now he was gone. Just like Shem.

Where were they?

"Where is he?" The words stuck in my throat, thick with emotion. "Where's his essence? Where's Shem's? Where are they?" Fresh seeds of panic took root inside me.

"If our earthly forms are destroyed, our essence returns home," Kabiel said. "A new earthly form is provided when it's time for us to walk the earth again. But with heaven's doors closed and God gone, Gabriel's essence will be trapped in between heaven and earth and eventually… eventually it will be lost."

"And Shem? He's there too? In between?"

"No, Rue. Shem was killed with a celestial sword. His essence was destroyed along with his earthly form."

A ball of pain pulsed in place of my heart. Shem was lost to me. Completely. Utterly. I took a shuddering breath riding the sharp wave of pain that rocked through me. Shem was gone but...but there was hope for Gabriel.

I needed to bring him back. "I fixed Gabriel's body though. So, he *can* come back. Why isn't he coming back?"

"He can't simply enter the vacated vessel," Asbeel said softly. "It doesn't work that way."

"We should have brought Erelim. He could have put him back."

"A reaper can't do that for a celestial," Asbeel said. "In the days of war, the celestials would share their name with a confidant, to be uttered only if their bodies fell because a true name can guide a celestial essence back to its body."

What did he mean? "His name is Gabriel."

"No. Gabriel is a word. A celestial's name is a melody. Every celestial has one unique to it," Asbeel said wistfully. "Watchers do not."

A melody...Wait...When we'd bonded, he'd kissed me, and I'd heard a melody. Could it be? Could that be his name? Hope ballooned inside me, shoving away the darkness that crowded my heart.

I squeezed my eyes shut and dragged the memory of that kiss, of that melody, to the surface of my mind. Its sweet notes filled my head and formed in my throat before springing to my lips.

Holding a tune wasn't a skill of mine, but it was as if this melody had been programmed into my vocal chords. It spilled free, rising in the air like a delicate scent.

My heart beat harder as the promise of something

unnamed bloomed inside me. Hope and yearning and forever more.

The melody rose and ebbed, coming to an end, but Gabriel remained unmoving and cold in my arms.

I needed to sing it again. But when I tried to summon the notes, they eluded me. Lost now. Used up. "No..." My voice cracked on a sob and then rage bubbled inside me, eating away at the sorrow because how dare he? How dare he break his word.

I tipped my head up to the sky, eyes burning with indignation. "You get your fucking ass back in this body right now, you hear me? You promised! You fucking promised you'd stay!" He lay still, unmoved by my plea, taunting me with this silence. "Damn you!" I slammed a fist onto his chest. "Damn you, you lying bastard!" I hit him again.

His body jerked on a gasp, eyes snapping open and gaze training in on my face. "What...what happened."

A manic laugh bubbled up my throat and I blinked back tears. "You fucking died, you ass. You died on me." I gathered him to me and squeezed. "But you came back."

He turned his head toward me, his breath warm against my collarbones. "I promised you that I'd stay, didn't I?"

I exhaled on a shaky laugh. "Yes, you did. You bloody did, so don't you dare try to check out again."

"Never." His voice was a reassuring rumble kissing my skin.

I closed my eyes and swallowed past the pinch in my throat, because almost losing him had made me realize that it was more than need that I felt for Gabriel. It was want.

I *wanted* him to stay.

I wanted him, and in this moment of pure relief and joy, there was no room for guilt.

CHAPTER 21

The angry skies were behind us, but we were still beneath thick gray clouds, as if this circle abhorred the sun. How was this circle so lush and green with such little sunlight? But then, I was assuming that the flora of this world needed the same sustenance as the flora of ours.

Kabiel walked ahead of us with Jilyana while Asbeel flew above us, scouting the terrain. The others fell behind a little, making up the rear. But I made sure to stay close to Gabriel. I'd almost lost him. I wasn't letting him out of my sight.

The chasm was a few minutes away, and then we'd be on the bridge and into the fifth circle.

We'd find the relic, and once we were in the fourth circle, Lucifer would find us.

I stole another glance at Gabriel. Did he look pale? Were those dark smudges under his eyes? Was he still hurt?

"I'm fine, Rue," Gabriel said. "You don't have to worry. Our bond allowed you to heal me fully."

Mention of the bond left me feeling strangely empty. "It's gone now, isn't it? The bond?"

"Yes." He looked relieved. "It's gone."

"You're relieved?"

"Aren't you?"

I should be, so why did I feel like I'd lost something vital?

"It'll take a little getting used to," Gabriel said. "It also means I won't be able to track you easily if we get separated."

"We won't get separated." I wouldn't allow it.

He glanced down at our joined hands. Had I done that? Taken his hand?

I made to let go, but he gripped my fingers, letting me know it was all right. Our gazes locked for a long beat, and something stirred in my chest, a sliver of warmth unfurling to wrap itself around my battered heart.

"It's huge!" Jilyana cried. "Look at it."

The moment was shattered because we were coming to the chasm—a split in the earth that stretched as far as the eye could see on either side of us.

Asbeel landed neatly in front of us. "There are several bridges crossing the chasm. Not that it matters, because we can fly."

"Any sign of the guardian?" Kabiel asked.

"Xelion said the guardian would be gone when the sun was at its peak, but the sky is overcast, and the world is gray, so it's hard to tell."

"We'll have to assume he's away for now," Kabiel said. "Let's cross."

We hurried to the nearest bridge stretching over the endless chasm, an aperture filled with mist, so it was impossible to tell how far it descended.

Kokabel launched himself into the air but made it barely four feet off the ground before crying out and dropping back to earth.

"What is it?" Asbeel asked.

Kokabel stretched his wings, then snapped them shut. "It hurts to fly."

Yomiel tried it with the same results. "There must be something in the air preventing flight to force the use of the bridge."

"Then we use the bridge," Kabiel said. "And we do it fast."

"Don't look down." Gabriel gave my hand a squeeze.

The bridge was a solid structure, steady beneath our feet and wide enough for three of us to walk side by side, so Kabiel and Gabriel flanked me, keeping me between them and away from the railings—barriers made of stone and shiny brown metal. Copper? No, that was too soft a metal. Gold? Softer still. It didn't matter; we were halfway across now. But the other side was a shimmery veil, making it impossible to determine what lay beyond. Thanatos had said something about it being a watery circle. But how watery? I couldn't swim. Had never learned. I'd have to hope that flying wouldn't be a problem in the fifth circle so that the watchers could carry me.

We were halfway across when a male materialized in front of us. He had to be at least eight feet tall and built to withstand a beating. His skin glowed with inner light, but his brown eyes held no fire.

"Passage is forbidden," he said wearily. "Please do not make me hurt you."

"We need to pass," Gabriel said. "Lucifer is waiting for us."

"Passage is forbidden," he said again, but this time his gaze flicked to something behind us.

Someone.

Another man stood behind us, watching us with angry eyes and a bitter smile. He wasn't as large as the one blocking our path, but there was an aura of lethality about him that made the hairs on my nape quiver. He said something in a gruff tongue, then doubled over in pain.

"What's happening? What's wrong?" Jilyana took a step toward him, but Asbeel pulled her back.

The groaning man said something else, his angry eyes now filled with remorse and fixed not on us but on the man blocking our path. He let out a final cry before bursting from his skin and morphing into a massive bird with a hooked beak.

He took to the air cawing loudly, the sound one of pain.

The large guy leapt off the bridge, body arching as it fell toward the mist. An invisible force grabbed him by his limbs so that he was spreadeagled, looking up at the sky emotionlessly as the bird swooped down toward him.

"Move!" Kabiel ordered us.

Gabriel pulled me away from the scene just as the bird buried the tip of its beak in the man's abdomen.

His agonized scream echoed in my ears as we ran across the bridge. The shimmering veil rushed to meet us, and we passed into a forest dotted with trees heavy with low-hanging purple fruits.

It took a moment to adjust to the sudden change of scene and for the caw of the bird and the man's gut-wrenching screams to stop echoing in my head. But then the man standing under the fruit-heavy trees came into focus.

He held a basket filled with the fruit and was staring at us in shock.

Wait...it was the man from the bridge, the one who'd turned into a bird.

"What is this?" Gabriel demanded. "You were on the bridge just now."

The man set his basket down and wiped his hands on his trousers, mumbling something in a language I didn't understand.

"We can't understand you," Kabiel said. He looked across at Asbeel. "Can you understand?"

"No," Asbeel said.

A figure emerged from deeper in the forest, large and golden—the other man from the bridge. But this version had life in his eyes and a smile on his face.

He didn't look surprised to see us and raised his hands, clapping them together a couple of times.

A fuzzy sensation passed through my brain.

"What did you do?" Gabriel demanded.

"I opened your minds," the bronze man said. "Now you'll be able to understand the many languages of Gehenna and be understood so that you may communicate with the people who inhabit this world."

Shit. I understood him. How the fuck had he done that?

He joined the smaller man and picked up the basket. "We've been expecting you for some time."

"I still can't believe it," the smaller man said.

Expecting us? "How could you know we'd be coming?"

He gave me a tired yet enigmatic smile. "Join us for lunch, and I'll tell you all about it."

My stomach chose that moment to growl.

"We'd be delighted," Gabriel said.

"Gabriel, we don't know who these men are," Kabiel reminded him.

"Ah, how remiss of me," the larger male said. "My name

is Prometheus, and this is my mate, Lorcan. I give you my word that we mean you no harm; in fact, we may be able to facilitate the task ahead of you. You can trust us."

My gut gave me no warning. No alarm bells. "Will your food be safe for a human?"

"Our food is safe for all." He beamed proudly.

"In that case, we'd love to join you for lunch."

Kabiel frowned but didn't protest as we followed the two men deeper into the forest.

I hoped my instinct wasn't leading me astray here, and when I squeezed Gabriel's hand, he shot me a look that echoed my thoughts.

We'd find out soon enough.

CHAPTER 22

Prometheus and Lorcan lived in a beautiful log cabin in the woods, surrounded by a neatly tended garden with a yard housing birds that resembled chickens and small grunting animals that reminded me of the pigs from our world.

Inside, the cabin was spacious but cozy. The ceilings were high to accommodate Prometheus's height, and the windows wide and tall to let in light and bathe the space in warmth.

The air was permeated with a delicious aroma coming from the huge pot simmering above the fire in the hearth.

"Lorcan's favorite stew," Prometheus said, following my gaze. "I make it for him frequently as it contains all the nutrients that his body needs."

"You enjoy it too," Lorcan said with a teasing smile.

"I do indeed," Prometheus said with a chuckle. "Even though I do not need the sustenance, and my indulging may be seen as gluttony."

"You're a god," Gabriel said.

"I am," Prometheus said without any kind of pride. "And Lorcan is immortal…because of me."

Lorcan put his hand on Prometheus's arm. "I'm glad of it."

"Of the punishment my indiscretion brought upon you?"

"I would suffer for an eternity with you rather than live a life of peace without you."

Prometheus leaned down to kiss his lover. "And so would I."

I needed to know what we'd seen on the bridge, how they were here, and why they'd known we were coming. "Was it you two on the bridge earlier?"

"Yes," Lorcan said. "And also no. The males on the bridge are remnants of our past. An imprint left behind after Thanatos freed us."

My confusion must have shown on my face because Lorcan quickly continued. "Let's eat, and Prometheus and I will tell you our story."

"And how you knew we were coming?" Kabiel added.

"That too."

Prometheus plodded to the kitchen and began to gather bowls and spoons. "Please find a seat. Our table isn't big enough for everyone, but there are chairs and plenty of floor space."

The next few minutes were spent filling bowls and finding places to sit. I claimed a spot on a bench by one of the windows, and Gabriel joined me. Jillian and Asbeel sat on the floor beside us, and the rest of the watchers found seats on the floor.

We ate in silence for a few moments. The stew was filling and flavorsome, the first hot meal I'd had in days, and my stomach was grateful for it.

Once spoons scraped bowls, Prometheus began to speak.

"You saw what happened on the bridge. You saw Lorcan turn into an eagle and tear out my heart?"

"Yes," Gabriel said.

"Then you saw our punishment." He paused for a moment as if gathering his thoughts. "That punishment was pressed on us by a jealous god who wanted me for herself. Her name is Zeus."

"Wait, I thought you were a god, too, so how could she punish you?"

"Even gods have a hierarchy. There are the first gods—the ancients. Then there are those of us who came later, born through their unions and dalliances or from experiments with the ether. We are *all* gods, but we do not all hold equal power. Zeus is one of the oldest. Neither feminine nor masculine, she is whatever she wishes to be at any given time, and her appetites are insatiable. I was her favorite toy, and for the pleasures I provided, she gave me certain freedoms. Such as being permitted to visit the worlds she created." Here he paused again, his gaze going misty as if he was falling into a memory, and when he continued to speak, his voice held a hypnotic quality, so it felt as if he was drawing us into the memory with him. "It was on one of those worlds that I met Lorcan. His people were a primitive breed—new and innocent, learning the wonders of life. They lived in darkness once the sun set. Unable to fend off the threats that lurked in the night.

"The first time I set eyes on Lorcan, he was huddled outside his shack, clutching a crudely made weapon—the chosen watcher for that night. He'd been frightened but determined. His aura was filled with love and light for his people. His courage was what drew me to him, but it was his beautiful mind that kept me." He looked across at Lorcan, who smiled, misty-eyed, urging him to continue with a nod.

"Zeus created Lorcan's world but did not give it fire. They had no light source. No way to stay warm in the winters. They had no way to cook their food to rid it of harmful bacteria, and predators did not fear them, hunting with impunity.

"I went back again and again to help them adapt. To help them find new ways to live, and in the process, I slowly fell in love with Lorcan. It soon became clear to me that Zeus had created this world as a twisted joke. That it wasn't meant to last long, but I wanted to protect it. I knew that Zeus could bar me from visiting Lorcan's world at any time. Knew that she had the power to keep me from him. I needed to ensure their safety if I could not return. And so, I did the only thing I could—I stole fire from Olympus."

"What do you mean you *stole* fire?" Kabiel asked.

"Hephaestus, the god of fire and flame, was a friend of mine, and so I went to him for help. He tried to convince me not to meddle, but I would not be swayed, and so he gave me an ember which would change Lorcan's world, and I, in turn, gave it to them. To their world. When Zeus discovered the truth, I hid Hephaestes's part in it and told her I'd stolen the ember. I thought I'd be punished for it by being grounded to Olympus, but I'd underestimated her obsession with me. She'd been spying on me. She knew about Lorcan. She'd wanted to see how far I'd fall to betray her, and she had a punishment prepared. One where we would forever be together and yet doomed to hurt one another."

The bridge? "Your punishment was to guard the chasm and be mutilated?"

"Yes," Prometheus said. "Lorcan would become an eagle and rip out my heart every day. And every night I would crush his skull between my hands. We were compelled to repeat the cycle and did so for millennia. Zeus would visit at first, to watch and revel in our pain, but after a while, she seemed to forget about us. But Thanatos would come visit often, and one day he said it was time to set us free. He broke whatever curse Zeus had placed on us and created a pocket of freedom for us here."

"Zeus was furious when she found out," Lorcan said with wide eyes. "She tried to curse us again but failed. Whatever Thanatos did protected us. But she was able to bar him from her circle. We haven't seen him since." He sat forward in his seat. "Did you go through the seventh circle? Did you see him?"

My heart sank. "We did. He helped us, and he...he was killed."

Prometheus let out a bark of laughter. "I'm sorry. I shouldn't laugh at your ignorance. Thanatos cannot be killed. None of the gods can. We are eternal. You saw the destruction of the vessel housing him, nothing more. He has not ceased to exist, and maybe you will see him one day again."

"That makes more sense," Gabriel said. "But what I don't understand is why Thanatos waited so long to free you."

"There are rules among the gods," Prometheus said. "Boundaries. Thanatos was merely adhering to them. He did what he could when the time was right."

"And what about us?" Kabiel asked. "How did you know to expect us? Thanatos? No. He was surprised to see us, and his vessel was destroyed on our way here so...who told you?"

"My brother Apollo came to visit us soon after we were freed from Zeus's control. He told me that we'd have visitors and that we should help them, that our world depended on it."

"How do you know he was talking about us?"

He looked right at me. "He showed me your face. Told me to trust it. I know you mean to cross the fifth circle, but unless you can swim for days or have the ability to breathe beneath the waters, you won't survive, and so we built you a vessel."

"A boat," Lorcan said, almost wistful. "It's magnificent, and it will get you to the gate that leads to the inner circles."

"Do you know where the gate is?" Jilyana asked.

"No, for that you will need to speak to the Gehennans who occupy the waters. You can lure them to the surface with blood."

"Blood?"

"They are carnivorous beings, so beware," Prometheus added. "Apollo told us that much. The rest...the rest is up to you."

"Come, we'll take you to it now," Lorcan said.

Prometheus chuckled indulgently. "Slow down, my sweet. They may wish to rest a little before they continue their journey."

I'd rested enough. The sooner we completed our quest, the better. "We're ready to go now."

"Then come." Prometheus led the way out of the cabin and into the afternoon light.

We took a pleasant trail through the forest with the sounds of nature around us and the smell of spring on the air. I'd taken my furs off in the cabin, and it was warm enough out here not to need them. Their pocket of existence was beautiful. Thanatos's doing. I was glad the god wasn't dead. That he continued to exist...somewhere.

The forest thinned, the trees growing sparser, and a shimmer bloomed in the distance.

"We're approaching the edge of our land," Lorcan said. "But look...look at what we built."

The boat came into view, a magnificent wooden structure larger than I would have expected with a mast and a sail and… "Does anyone here know how to drive one of these things?"

"Sail," Kabiel said with a chuckle. "You do not drive a boat, you sail it, and yes, I spent some time on the seas in one of my sojourns on earth."

His nostalgic tone hinted at stories to be told, and I promised the nosy bitch inside me that we'd find out one day.

"We had plenty of time to work on it," Prometheus said. "In fact, it's been a labor of love." He put his arm around Lorcan, and they both looked up at the boat as if it was their child.

And in a way, it was.

They'd brought it into being together, after all.

"We'll take good care of it," Gabriel said. "It's truly beautiful."

"Oh, you haven't seen anything yet," Lorcan said. "We put in bunks, and there's a cubby for storage, and we built a latrine at the back to allow for privacy."

"Yes, I would not have thought of those details alone," Prometheus said, a proud glint in his eyes. "Come inside." He led the way up the ladder that leaned up against the boat. "This will be your home for the next few days, after all."

"Days?" Jilyana said. "How long does it take to get to the fourth circle?"

"The fifth is vast," Prometheus said. "Thanatos once told us it would take four suns to reach the fourth circle."

Four days. We'd already been gone two. We still had to locate the relic, so that would add time to our journey. How long would we be stuck in Gehenna?

My thoughts took a backseat as we climbed onto the boat, and the next few minutes were spent exploring. I'd never been on a boat. Never seen one, so there was a lot to take in. Words like deck, stern, bow, helm, rudder. They all melted into one. Thank goodness the watchers knew what Prometheus was talking about. They'd sailed before, built boats before. Been on the sea before.

Thank fuck they'd come with us because Gabriel wasn't as up to speed with how to sail.

There were three rooms below—a small seating area, a sleeping area, and a kitchen that housed a small stove filled with fuel called coal.

"We'll bring you supplies," Lorcan said. "They should last you for your trip. You'll need fresh water too. We'll fill containers of it."

"And how do we get the boat into the water?" Kabiel asked.

Lorcan looked up at Prometheus, who smiled smugly. "I may have been cursed, but I did not lose my godly strength. The sea lies beyond this veil. Once you are prepared to leave, I will push the vessel through the veil and onto the sea."

"In that case, let's prepare," Gabriel said.

It didn't take long for us to load up the ship with supplies, although I felt bad taking food from Prometheus and Lorcan's stores, but they were adamant they had enough and could get more if need be. The world that Thanatos had created for them here was bountiful.

The sky was a beautiful orange hue by the time we were ready to leave, and the immortal lovers prepared to disembark.

I joined them at the ladder. "Thank you, for everything."

"Thank us by fixing this broken world," Lorcan said. "We may only have a sliver of it, but it's our home."

"But even if you fail," Prometheus said, "even if our world is doomed, we're grateful for the time we had together."

The way they looked at each other, pure and unfettered by all the horror they'd experienced, made my heart ache.

Gabriel pulled up the ladder once Prometheus and Lorcan were on the ground.

Kabiel took the helm, and the other watchers perched on the bow and stern. Jilyana stayed close to Asbeel, looking out at the veil from the bow.

Prometheus and Lorcan waved goodbye before walking out of sight, and in the next moment, the boat was inching toward the veil. It swallowed Jilyana and Asbeel first, slowly eating away at the boat until it was rushing toward us, and for a moment, doubt and fear dug their claws into me, but Gabriel took my hand, and the fear melted.

"We've got this," he said as the shimmer washed over us.

I hoped so, because we had so much more riding on finding the last piece of the relic now. With two worlds hanging in the balance, failure wasn't an option.

CHAPTER 23

BASTIAN

"How much farther?" Bee asks from the seat behind me.

"We should be at the coordinates in five miles."

"So close."

She sounds worried. Nervous.

I get it. So am I.

This is the first journey where we haven't been attacked by the monsters, and it feels like our luck should be running out, but we're almost at base zero, so maybe we'll make it without mishap.

The people on our bus are silent now. The constant low hum of conversation has died as if they're also experiencing the same fears and doubts as me.

We'd be delusional not to be worried. Not to doubt. Not to wonder when the sky will open and spit out razor beaks or when crabines might burst out of the ground.

This silence isn't normal. It feels ominous, like the eerie calm before a vicious storm.

Bee crouches beside me, her hand on the arm of my chair, her eyes on the road ahead, scanning the terrain, always scanning.

"Bee, sit down. The watchers have got this."

They're in the air above us and running along the ground ahead and behind us. They have our backs, and there's no need to worry. Two miles off now.

The ground is flat and dry here, stretching as far as the eye can see either side of us. We're exposed to attack. I glance in the rear-view at the bus behind us driven by Derry, a guy I'd never spoken to until last night.

Derry is one of the old-timers, in his fifties, and used to drive a lorry. He has all the supplies in his bus along with a handful of passengers.

"We should be coming up on those coordinates any second."

"I don't see anything," she says.

"Gabriel said they're underground."

"So we need to look for a hatch? A sewer pipe? What do—"

"Bee, what is it? What's...Oh..." The sky ahead is a churning black mass of tendrils like the other day when our bus was upended by monsters that appeared out of nowhere. The same inky shit that misted the skies all day. It's Gehenna bleeding into our world, which means—

Tumiel appears in our path, wings beating hard to stay airborne. "Slow it down!" he orders before shooting up to join the other watchers.

I decelerate, and Derry takes his lead from me until we're moving ten miles an hour. Razor beaks spawn to life in the sky amidst the black swirly shit, and the watchers and reapers attack them.

"We have eight razor beaks," Bee says. "Maybe more."

"They've taken down three." We're getting too close now, so I slow down even more. "We need to let them handle this."

"You say that as if I'm begging to go out there and help. Heck, I'm not suicidal."

Five down. "We have the numbers, so we should—"

A sound like the crack of lightning cuts the air followed by another and another, and one of the razor beaks falls out of the air.

It takes a moment for my brain to comprehend what's just happened because it's been a long time since I've heard this sound, and even then, I only ever heard it in movies.

"What is it? What's happening?" Bee demands.

"Gunfire." My heart hammers in my throat. "Someone is shooting at the raptors."

"Base zero?"

"It has to be." I find the source of bullets a moment later —raised hatches in the ground with the barrels of guns pointed into the air. "There! To the left. Do you see them?"

"They must have eyes on the area," Bee says. "They know we're incoming. They're helping us."

We're almost under the battle when the gunfire turns on the watchers.

"They're shooting our people!" Bee sounds incredulous, and I'm incensed for a moment until it hits me. They don't know the watchers are with us. To them, the watchers are monsters just like the razor beaks.

"Open the door!" Bee orders. "I have to stop them."

The last razor beak is down, but the gunfire continues, aimed at the watchers, who desperately try to avoid the bullets that might not kill them but could seriously hurt them, leading to days or maybe weeks of recovery.

We need them.

We need all the muscle we have. I flip the lever to let Bee out. We're not going fast enough to cause her any damage as she leaps out and runs toward the fallen beaks, arms waving in the air to get the hidden operatives' attention.

"Stop. Stop! They're with us!" she yells so loudly I can hear her over the engine, but can they hear her over the bullets?

Fuck. I swerve off the road and bring the vehicle to a halt.

I'm out the door and running toward her, yelling for the gunfire to stop. No heroics Rue had said, but this is Bee. I can't let her be hurt.

The earth trembles, and a screech batters my eardrums as a crabine bursts out of the ground to our left.

I barely have time to grab hold of Bee when it rushes us. My stomach drops, heart fit to burst because there is no escape.

The gunfire ceases for a beat, allowing the whoosh of wings to rise above everything, and Bee and I are suddenly surrounded by watchers, their wings flared like protective shields.

Gunfire explodes outside our cocoon of safety, and then silence reigns. The only sound is that of our breath and the rush of blood in my veins.

The watchers step away to release us, and a quick scan shows that the guns are gone.

"Bee?" Tumiel sounds odd, his voice strained as he reaches for her.

"Tumiel?" Bee holds his hand as he buckles. I grab him but almost lose my grip because his torso is coated in something wet and warm. The coppery scent of blood hits me. No...Oh no.

I hit the ground with my knees, cradling his limp body.

Blood coats my hands, bubbling out of the wound in his chest.

He's been shot.

"No. NO!" Bee cups his face. "Tumiel. Wake up. Wake up. You have to heal. You have to heal!"

Rage blooms inside me. "He's one of us! One of us, and you shot him!" Bee clutches Tumiel, sobbing and mumbling at him to wake up as I stand and stride toward the spot where I know the hatches are housed.

"Calm." Erelim places his hand on my shoulder. "They are protecting themselves. If we want sanctuary, we must not be viewed as a threat."

With Bee's sobs echoing in my ears and an image of my friend's glassy eyes in my head, it takes every ounce of my will to push down my indignant rage.

"We're with Gabriel." I rattle off the code. "Gabriel sent us here for sanctuary. There are people on the bus. Supplies. Food. The creatures with us are called watchers. They're celestials on our side." I take a breath, suddenly so weary that standing up is an effort. "Please. Let us in. I can tell you what's happened and why Gabriel hasn't been in touch recently."

The ground rumbles, and an area several feet behind the gun hatches opens.

A voice booms out. "Humans only. Your celestials can wait until we have spoken to you."

"We have an injured watcher here. He's...He's my friend." My voice cracks. "Please, we need medical attention."

Silence greets me for several beats. "You may bring the

injured watcher inside. All other non-humans must remain above ground."

"It's fine," Erelim says. "We'll be fine up here. Take the humans in."

My shoulders sag. This will have to be enough for now. "We accept your terms."

CHAPTER 24

RUE

The sea wasn't so bad. Two days in and we'd had steady winds and a calm surface to journey through. The relic was close and getting closer. I'd felt it as soon as I'd passed through the veil, and opening the channel had made that connection stronger.

Jilyana kept the relics shielded to allow me to maintain a lock on the fourth piece. The first day I'd had to keep opening the channel to make sure we were headed in the right direction, but now the relic's presence was a steady vibration, calling to me.

I stood on the bow, looking out at the vast expanse of rippling gray and green. This circle was truly nothing but water, and although we'd spotted small outcrops of land, they'd been dry lumps of rock jutting out of the waves. So far, we hadn't come across any Gehennans, and we hadn't tried to lure any to the surface with blood either. Once we got to the location of the relic, we might have no choice but to get some assistance.

With so little land to speak of, it was logical to assume that the relic was on the seabed—somewhere we wouldn't be able to go. We had to hope the Gehennans of this circle were as helpful as the other circles.

I sensed Gabriel's presence before he spoke. Our bond was gone, but the connection we'd developed remained. In fact, it was stronger now than before, and I wasn't sure what to make of that except...I liked it.

I liked that we were on the same wavelength. That he seemed to know what I was thinking most of the time. I liked sharing a bunk with him and falling asleep with the sound of his heartbeat against my ear. I liked it all a little too much.

"Jilyana says food is ready," Gabriel said finally. "We're close to the relic, aren't we?"

"Yes. It's so strong now. I think...maybe tomorrow, if not tonight..."

"Good. Then we should all get some rest." He glanced down the boat toward the helm, where Kabiel kept his hand on the wheel, steadying our course. "He needs to rest. Asbeel can take the wheel for a while, but Kabiel needs to relinquish it."

Kabiel had barely left the helm the past two days. Although the other watchers claimed they could steer the boat just as well, he wouldn't let any of them take control for more than an hour at a time. Every time he took back the helm, he'd check with me to ensure we were headed in the right direction.

Gabriel was right; Kabiel needed to take a longer break. "I'll speak to him."

"Good. He'll listen to you." Gabriel squeezed my shoulder. "I'll see you downstairs."

I turned away from the late afternoon sun and crossed

the deck to climb the steps to the helm where Kabiel stood, legs shoulder width apart, hands on the wheel.

"Do we need to change direction?" he asked.

"No. You need to take a break."

"I don't need a break."

"Then humor me."

He snorted softly. "Why?"

"Why not?"

"Because I'd rather be up here than down there watching you and Gabriel cuddle." He said it in such an even tone that it took me a moment to register the meaning of his words.

"Why does it bother you?"

"You know why."

I did. I fucking did, but I didn't want to think about it. I couldn't cope with more feelings right now. Him wanting to fuck me at one point I could handle. But nothing more than that. I didn't have the emotional space for it.

"Kabiel, I—"

"I know. I don't expect anything from you. But allow me to deal with my unwelcome yearnings in my own way."

I wasn't about to push him right now. If this helped him cope, then so be it. "If you get tired, you need to switch with Asbeel. Promise me."

"I'm not a fool, Rue. I know my limits."

So abrasive. So like Shem. I backed away.

There was only one Shem, and he was gone. "I'll have some food sent up for you."

He made a noncommittal sound, and I forced myself to walk away. I couldn't get tangled up in his emotional turmoil. My heart was bruised and tired, and Gabriel understood that. He didn't push. He didn't ask for anything.

Gabriel was the calm in the eye of the storm, and that's where I needed to stay for now.

I joined the others below deck to find Jilyana passing around bowls of soup. Soup and stew were the staples of our journey so far. Filling and easy to prepare.

"No Kabiel?" Gabriel asked as I took the vacant spot beside him at the table.

"No. But he'll let us know if he needs relieving."

I took the bowl Jilyana offered, aware of Gabriel's hot, probing gaze on the side of my face.

He didn't push me for more information, though. Although I was sure he'd ask me what had been said later.

Nothing got past Gabriel, not when it came to me, and there was comfort in that. Comfort in not always having to find the words. In having someone who simply felt what you did.

What would this have felt like with the bond in place? What kind of connection would we have had if we'd opened ourselves to it?

Why did it even matter?

"Eat up," Gabriel said. "I'll take some food up to Kabiel."

He filled a bowl and clomped up the steps.

"It's different here," Yomiel said. "The devolution is slower."

"It's because we're close to Rue," Asbeel said. "Rue, the relics, and the residual power."

"We're close now, aren't we?" Jilyana said. "I felt something today. A prickle of awareness."

She'd finally sensed it too. "Yes. We're close. I think late tonight or early tomorrow."

"Then we should be ready to set down anchor," Kokabel said.

"And feed blood to the waves," Matarel added. "The relic

will be far below us. We must hope we can convince a Gehennan to aid us."

"To think that there's a whole world down there," Jilyana said. "A world where the inhabitants breathe water."

It was a fantastical thought, but then I was sure the humans of my world would have said the same thing if someone told them that celestials existed and that we were about to be invaded by monsters. Anything was fantastical until it happened, and then...then it quickly become the norm. Mundane. Life.

I drank my soup, barely tasting it as nerves spawned in my belly.

We'd been supremely lucky so far. With Thanatos, the village of Gehennans in the sixth circle, and Prometheus and Lorcan's help, we'd gotten this far—so close to the relic that I could almost see it in my mind's eye. So close that I could almost feel the weight of it in my hands.

So close...

But everything could be thwarted if the Gehennans of this realm refused to help us.

And that...that scared the shit out of me.

CHAPTER 25

GABRIEL

Kabiel's wings flex as I approach, a clear protective sign, which means that whatever was said between him and Rue is enough to put him on the defensive.

I hold out the bowl. "You should eat."

"Set it to one side and say what you came to say."

"I didn't come to say anything. I came to listen."

"I have nothing to say to you, Gabriel. It's obvious you feel that you can fill the void that Shem's death has left in her life."

A wave of disgust washes over me. "The fact that you think in that way is the very reason Rue will hold you at arm's length. Rue isn't a prize to be won or a battle to be fought. She's a woman who's grieving. What she needs the most are friends."

"Friends that sleep in the same bed as her."

"If need be."

"And you want nothing from her?"

"I want her to be happy. To be safe. To heal. And once those things happen, then I will think about all the other things I may want."

He's silent for the longest time. "I wish I was as noble as that."

"You can only be yourself, Kabiel. But if you care for her, then you'll find the strength to put her needs before your own, especially now."

He lets out a bark of laughter. "Easy for you to say with your perfect skin and perfect smile. But me...Look at me. I'm a fucking monster, the kind that makes her shudder in revulsion despite what she claims." His words tip into a growl of frustration, then silence for several frustrated beats. "I've been lost for so long, hungering only for celestial light and flesh that this...this new hunger is tearing me apart."

He speaks of hunger and want, but I doubt he knows what it is he truly craves. "The hunger for what exactly? For Rue's love and affection or for what Shem had?"

"What do you mean?"

"Is it Rue that you want or are you craving how her loving you could make you feel like less of a monster?"

"I...I don't know."

"Then you must step back and take the time to find out. Rue's heart is bruised and battered enough. She's lost one male she loves and will soon lose another. I won't allow anyone to play with her emotions. Not now. Not ever."

"You were willing to hand her into my care when you thought you were dying."

"If I had died, you wouldn't be up here procrastinating. The full weight of responsibility would be on your shoulders. Everything would be different, and you know it."

His eyes narrow. "You think you're the only one whose feelings for Rue are real?"

"No, Kabiel. But I do think your feelings haven't been tested enough for you to know what they mean. But the time will come, and you'll know for certain."

I put my hand on the wheel. "Eat now. I'll hold the wheel steady."

He locks gazes with me for a second before inclining his head and relinquishing the helm to me.

He eats, and I look out at the rapidly darkening sky. I'm here for a reason. Brought back by Rue calling my true name, into a body healed by the Morningstar power for a reason, because no matter what anyone thinks, that power should not have healed my body. Not even with the bond in place.

Lucifer allowed it to heal me.

She changed the rules.

She wants me watching over Rue. Which confirms that even though Rue may not be bonded to me, she is mine to protect, body and soul. Not just because of my vow to Shem, but because Lucifer herself wills it.

Yes, Lucifer wants Rue alive for now, but what happens when Rue's served her purpose?

I must be ready to protect her, and I'll need Kabiel on my side to help me.

KABIEL

Guilt is an emotion alien to me. Even before my devolution, guilt remained elusive. But I feel it now.

Gabriel's words resonate in my head.

Am I coveting Rue or what she represents?

Shame heats my blood when I recall the many nights I

watched her sleep. Wanting. Wishing it was me pressed against her body and not Shem.

Wishing it was my body she caressed with such tenderness, not his.

Is it Rue that I crave, or the acceptance she represents?

To feel wanted again.

To feel loved.

To feel...humanity's touch.

Yes, I've missed that. Missed walking among humans and being accepted. Loved. Wanted. That was the beauty of my watcher life. The beauty of not being a monster.

Is that all Rue represents to me?

A gust of wind hits the sails, and I grip the wheel tighter, holding it steady. The world ahead blurs.

Is that fog?

Yes. Thick, soupy fog.

My gut tightens in warning.

"Kabiel!" Kokabel shouts from the bow. "I think we should drop the sails."

"Do it!"

He and Yomiel scramble to bring the sails down as we move ever closer to the ominous fog.

I grab the rope attached to the helm and tie off the wheel to hold it in place before leaping onto the deck to help them.

We're almost done, and the ship is slowing.

But then the night is filled with song.

I want to listen.

I must listen.

CHAPTER 26

RUE

I helped Jilyana strap the relic bundle to her chest for bed because the only way for her to shield them was to keep them in contact with her body. It was awkward, and I was so grateful to her for doing it. Sleeping with them strapped to her couldn't be comfortable.

"Is that okay?" I tightened the scarf that bound them to her.

"Yes. That should hold."

"But is it too tight? Should I loosen it?"

She turned to me with a smile. "I'm fine, Rue. Honestly. I'm just glad I can help."

"I'm glad you're here."

Being on a boat fueled by testosterone would have been unbearable without Jilyana. We'd spent a lot of time together the past two days. Talking. About her life in the djinn world. About my life at base. About Bastian and Bee and...and about Shem. Yes, it was nice to have someone to talk to about him. Someone who'd loved him. Someone who was heartbroken like me.

We'd bonded, and I'd trust this woman with my life.

"Shall I make us some herbal tea before bed?" Jilyana asked.

"I'll do it. You cooked."

I turned to the stove as an awful screech shattered the silence.

Jilyana grabbed my arm. "What is that?"

The screech came again, longer this time.

Gabriel emerged from the back room. "What is that?"

His expression was enraptured, his eyes glazed.

"I need it," Asbeel said from behind him. "It's so beautiful."

"I think I know what this is," Jilyana said. "We can't let them onto the deck. Help me get them into the back room."

We worked together to shove the males into the back room. They resisted a little but didn't fight us. Jilyana locked the door.

"It won't hold them for long," she said. "The louder it gets, the more they'll want to go to it."

"What is it?"

"A siren song. Vicious creatures that live in the sea who lure sailors to their death. I learned of the myth a long time ago. I guess in Gehenna the myths are real."

Another screech. Louder this time.

Thud. Thud.

Gabriel and Asbeel wanted out but… "Kabiel and the others!"

We rushed up the steps and onto the deck, which had been claimed by night. The screeching was so loud out here that it rattled my brain, making it hard to focus on my thoughts.

How the fuck was this a song? And where was the bow?

"The fog!" Jilyana said. "They're in the fog."

But if we were headed this way, then it meant the relic was also in the fog. The helm was unmanned.

My heart sank. "Kabiel! Kabiel!"

Matarel crawled out of the fog, moving slowly across the deck toward us. His eyes held wild fire. "Help. Me."

Shit! We rushed forward and flanked him, guiding him to the door that led below deck. "Get him into the room with the others."

Jilyana nodded, and I turned back to the fog. "Kabiel!" I hurried forward, pulse pounding in my throat. "Kabiel!"

He staggered out of the fog, dragging Kokabel across the ground by his leg, while Yomiel was slung over his shoulder.

"Help. Me," he bit out.

I grabbed his arm, noting the tension in his muscles and the stilted movement of his legs, as if he was forcing them to move away from the fog with all his will.

"I. Can't. It's too strong," he growled.

"You can. Kabiel, you can." We were almost at the steps when he jerked away from us, swinging his body around toward the fog.

"No!" I grabbed him. "Kabiel, no. Listen to me. Listen to my voice."

He came to a standstill, eyes squeezed shut, teeth clenched as he fought the siren song.

I grabbed his face and pressed my lips to his and opened the channel to the Morningstar power. I wasn't sure if it would help, but I needed to do something.

He gasped, mouth parting against mine so our breath mingled for a moment. His skin softened to silky smooth beneath my fingertips, and the tension in his jaw melted.

"I'm here," Kabiel said. "I'm here, Rue."

I broke the connection and pulled. "It worked."

"I can hear it, but it's not as compelling any longer." He looked at the fog. "The relic is in there, isn't it?"

"Yes. We have no choice but to go through it. But I have a plan."

THE MORNINGSTAR POWER seemed to help calm the watchers, making it easier for them to resist the siren song that to Jilyana and me, sounded like nails on a chalkboard.

"We can't stay here while you go out there alone," Gabriel said after I relayed our plan.

"You're a liability out there right now. All of you are. If Jilyana is right, then the creatures out there want you because you're male. They don't want me or Jilyana. We can steer the ship through the fog, and if those things attack, then we can use the Morningstar power to defend ourselves."

Asbeel moved to the door as if in a daze, and Jilyana pulled him away from it. "Please," she said. "Please stay hidden."

"I don't like this," Gabriel said. "I don't like you doing this alone." But his tone said he knew that we had no other choice.

"We need that relic piece, and if it's in the fog, we can find it. If not, then we can steer us through. We can do this."

To make doubly sure they stayed put, we pulled the downy stuffing out of a pillow and used it to block their ears. Hopefully the injection of Morningstar power plus the ear plugs would be enough to keep them safe.

We locked them below deck and hurried back up into

the night. A lock wouldn't keep them penned in if they were determined to be free, but it made me feel better.

The boat continued to inch forward, despite the sails being down, and the fog had eaten away half of it.

Jilyana took my hand. "We can do this."

"Yes. We can."

The fog sucked us in, washing over us until it was all around us, until we were in the thick of it and the screeching was all I could hear.

"I wish they'd stop," Jilyana said. "It's so loud."

It *was* loud, and it was getting on my nerves. If they thought they were getting their fins on my watchers, then they were mistaken.

"Hey! Stop it. Stop fucking screaming!"

Something hit the side of the ship to my left. Then something else thudded against the right.

A scrambling sound followed as the creatures climbed up onto our boat.

"Are you ready, Jilyana?"

She nodded. "I am."

Several shadowy figures landed on the deck around us with wet sounds. I caught the impression of yawning mouths and eerie green eyes before I opened the channel to the Morningstar power. Jilyana pushed out her hand, sending a jet of dark energy toward the nearest creature. It screamed as the power hit it, then exploded into white glowing cinders.

Another one rushed forward, and we blasted that too, then a third and a fourth.

A shrill scream tore through the night, the pitch like needles to my eardrums, almost making me lose my connection to the power.

The creatures stopped attacking us and backed away.

This wasn't our doing. This was because of the scream. The command. Yep, something was coming. Something more powerful. Something that these fuckers obeyed.

The mist parted and thinned as a tall, painfully thin figure stepped out of it. Flowing dark locks floated around its frame as if each tendril was alive. This creature had a feminine energy with skin as white as bone and large dark eyes that reminded me of an abyss, desperate to swallow me and keep me. Her mouth was a thin line that extended almost from ear to ear. The top half of her body was stark white skin threaded with a network of black veins, and the bottom half was scaly, like the tail of a fish. She glided toward us on tentacles that moved across the deck like slippery spider legs.

My stomach knotted with terror, but I held my ground. "Get off my ship. Now. You're not welcome here."

She hissed, showcasing so many teeth that my heart almost stopped. "These are my waters. And all that pass belong to me." The words held a bubbling quality that made my stomach ache with fear.

I tamped down on the terror, injecting authority into my tone. "Not this ship. And not us. But, hey, if you want to die, then stick around. We can make that happen."

Her gaze flicked to the dead bodies of her minions, then back to us. "We are many."

"Yeah? Good, more for me to kill, then. Trust me, my power isn't going to run out."

Her eyes narrowed as she considered the odds, and there was intelligence in that look. This was more than a predator.

When she spoke, her tone slipped into a conversational one. "You speak our tongue. You wield strange power. You are not Gehennan."

"No. We're travelers from another world, and we're here

on an important mission, so you can either get out of our way, help us, or die. Your choice."

"There has not been a ship in our waters for decades. Not since the lands were swallowed by the sea. Before that, the Gehennans would provide offerings to pass through our lands. Several offerings every month. The sweet flesh of the betrayer. We hunger now, and you have cargo filled with sweet flesh. Give us the males, and you may pass unchallenged and with our protection."

"Protection from what? From being attacked by you? No thanks. And those males aren't cargo. They're my friends. You can't have them. So for the last time, get out of our way, help us, or die. Pick one. Now."

"Wait," Jilyana said. "Listen, even if we gave you the males—"

I squeezed her hand sharply. "What are you doing?"

She shook her head. "Trust me." Then to the tentacle woman, "Even if we gave you the males, what then? You'd be starving again soon enough. There won't be any more ships. Any more offerings. Your world is broken. But we can fix it. That's why we're here."

Her eyes narrowed. "Something is wrong with our world..."

She sensed it too.

"Yes," Jilyana continued. "There are fractures in your world, and in ours. These fractures have disrupted the balance of your world. That's why the seas swallowed the land which forced the Gehennans to leave."

Jilyana had the tentacle woman's attention. She'd defused this situation, and hope bloomed in my chest. "If you want to fix things, if you want the ships back, then you need to help us. Help us to fix this, and everything can go back to how it was. You can have your regular offerings again. You won't have to starve."

"You can make the ships return? You can fix this?" the woman asked.

I had no clue if fixing things would mean the Gehennans returned, but fuck it. "Yes. I can."

The creatures began to mutter amongst themselves.

"Silence!" their leader snapped. "How will you fix it?"

She wasn't stupid. She wanted details. I was happy to give them to her. "I can seal the fractures and allow your world, and mine, to heal. But I need something. Something that fell into your circle two decades ago. A fragment of an important relic. Have you seen it?"

The creatures started to murmur again, and this time the leader took a little longer to hush them. Finally, she raised her hand, and they quietened.

"Something glows on the shores of Perinady," she said. "Perinady was once a city, and now all that remains is a strip of land leading to the gate."

"The gate to the fourth circle?"

"Yes. But that strip of land is now home to the Ioness. They nest there now. I believe this light, this...*relic* is what has drawn them. They guard it. They...worship it. They will not let you claim it."

"They won't have a choice."

Her eyes gleamed like wet stones. "In the beginning, I sent my people to investigate. We retrieved their dead bodies from the waters offshore. But maybe you will fare differently and this world will be healed. If not, then we will retrieve the bodies of your cargo and have our feast."

A win-win situation for her, it seemed. "Can you lead us to Perinady?"

"It seems your ship is bound toward it anyway. But I will

clear the mist so that you may see your path. We'll be watching, and if you go off course, you will hear our cries." She didn't wait for my confirmation before turning away from us and walking into the mist.

The other creatures leapt into the water. After a few moments, the fog parted, clinging to the sides of the boat but leaving our path clear.

Jilyana sagged, hand on her chest. "We did it."

"*You* did it, Jilyana. I was ready to battle, but you reasoned with her. Thank you."

She dropped her gaze and shook her head. "I just...I want to help. I need to fix things. To atone."

"And you will. We're so close." The relic called to me. "It's so close now."

Jilyana frowned and dragged me toward the bow. "Rue, is that...is that land?"

A strip of gray sat on the surface of the sea in the distance. "Yes...yes it is."

CHAPTER 27

We'd expected to be sailing for four days, but barely three days after we'd set sail, land was in sight. The relic and the gate were close. My stomach fizzed with excitement and apprehension. What were these Ioness creatures like? How many of them would we be up against?

No one would say it, but we were all exhausted. The last week had taken a toll on us, and even the past two days on the ship hadn't been enough to recharge us.

But once Lucifer had all the relic pieces, we'd pass the baton to her. The last leg of this race would be hers, and we could go to base zero and wait for her to restore the balance.

"I can see them in the water," Asbeel said from the bow. "Those creatures that wanted to eat us are following the ship."

"Of course they are," Gabriel said. "They're hoping we'll die and end up in the water so they can feast."

But that wasn't the impression I'd gotten. "I think, if they have a choice, they'd like their circle to go back to the way it was. To be populated. To have the status quo restored. Eating us would be a consolation prize."

Silence fell, the only sound the whoosh of the sea as the strip of land grew closer. Kabiel hadn't bothered taking the helm. We were headed in the right direction, after all. Instead, he stood beside me, arms crossed, watching the rapidly incoming shoreline.

"We'll have to drop the anchor soon," Kokabel said. "We'll fly the rest of the way."

There was a small boat tied to the side of the ship, but I didn't relish being so close to the waves, despite the strange tentacle woman's promise.

"I see a light," Yomiel said from the air. "I don't see any creatures, but the land has many small hills. The light comes from within."

"We're close enough," Kabiel said. "Release the anchor."

The rattle of chains as the anchor was released was followed by a loud splash as it hit the water. The ship came to a halt, bobbing in place as we gathered our party.

Jilyana held on to the backpack, but Gabriel took the bat.

"I'll carry Rue," Gabriel said to Kabiel. "You need your talons free to fight if need be."

But I could fight too. "Jilyana and I can fight as well. We can blast any threat that stands between us and the relic."

"Then I'll make sure we stay close to you," Asbeel said, holding his arms out to Jilyana.

We took to the air and approached the land in a V formation with Kabiel at the helm. I caught the streamlined dark shapes of the siren creatures in the water swimming toward land, but they stopped where the water grew shallow, heads bobbing above the surface to watch as we arched through the sky aiming for the beach.

This high up, it was easy to spot the glow on land. It peeked out from between jutting mounds of rock.

My blood heated, chest burning with awareness even though the door to the power was closed.

This fragment was powerful, and so far, the terrain was clear. No Ioness guarding it. The tentacle woman must have old intel.

We flew over the rocks, and a glowing crater was visible. The relic was in it. It had to be.

We landed beside the crater, which was surrounded by the rocky mountains.

"I don't see any threat," Jilyana said. "But we should hurry."

"Agreed," Gabriel said. "I'll take Rue down and—"

The ground trembled, and the sand shifted to swallow our boots. I grabbed hold of Gabriel as we both lost our balance. His wings flared to catch us and keep us upright.

Jilyana cried out from behind me, and Asbeel called her name.

The rocks around us shook and began to rise, and my pulse hammered in my throat because the rocks weren't rocks: They were huge shells. Shells set on top of massive crab-like creatures.

"I think we just found the Ioness," Kabiel called out. "Gabriel, get Rue and Jilyana to the relic. We'll hold them off."

I turned, wild-eyed, searching for Jilyana.

She was a few feet away in Asbeel's arms.

I reached for her, but my path was interrupted as a jet of light lanced out of the crater. It bounced off an Ioness's shell and hit Kokabel in the chest.

He was thrown several feet away and landed on his ass.

His chest was charred, and he coughed up blood, hand going to the wound.

"Kokabel!" Yomiel rushed forward but was intercepted by another jet of light. It hit another Ioness and missed Kabiel by a mere foot.

"It's the relic!" Jilyana said. "It's protecting itself. We have to get to it. We have to show it that it belongs with us."

The Ioness roared and advanced as more streams of light exploded out of the crater.

"Evade!" Kabiel yelled. "Get Rue and Jilyana to the relic!"

Gabriel dropped the bat, then grabbed me with one arm and Jilyana with the other before diving into the crater with us.

His wings shot out, catching air. We swerved to avoid a blast of light, then again to avoid another, rising then diving to avoid being hit.

But this was the relic.

This was a connection to the Morningstar.

It was awake somehow.

Alive somehow.

Which meant I could connect to it.

I opened the channel and allowed the Morningstar power to fill me. "Drop me."

"What?" Gabriel asked incredulously.

"Drop me into the light."

"That's insane."

"It's the only way. Do it. Do it now!"

"Do it!" Jilyana urged. "She's right. It needs to feel her. It needs to feel what we represent to know we're not a threat."

"Fuck!" Gabriel kissed my temple. "If you die..."

"Then find me in the afterlife." We flew toward the center of the crater. "Drop me! Now!"

He released me with a curse.

The light swallowed me whole.

I was no longer falling.

I was no longer afraid.

This was peace and bliss.

This was home.

The light filled me, reading me. Finding its haven through me. It communicated without words, telling me that it had waited so long, that it was so lonely and was ready to go home.

"Rue? Rue, can you hear me?" Gabriel pulled me out of the light. "Rue, wake up!"

My eyes snapped open to find everyone standing around me. Jilyana clung to Asbeel, and Yomiel braced Kokabel, whose abdomen was no longer wounded. Kabiel was unharmed too. Good. This was good.

"You got it." Kabiel's gaze dropped to my chest, where I clutched the relic from the crater.

I'd found it.

The light and then… "What…what happened?"

"You fell into the light, then you floated out of it, clutching the relic. It glowed for a little while and so…so did you."

It had spoken to me. It had been alive but now…now that consciousness was gone. Where had it gone?

"We have to move," Kabiel said. "The Ioness seem to have backed off, but who knows, they might change their minds."

He was right. They'd been somehow controlled by the relic for decades. Protecting it. Now they were free, and we could very well be food to them. "The gate? We need to find it."

"Already did," Yomiel said. "It's a portal. A vortex suspended in the air."

"Take me to it."

Gabriel helped me up, and we hurried past the stationary Ioness and across the sand. Several heads bobbed far from shore, dark hair gleaming in the moonlight.

"They're watching," Kabiel said. "No food for you today...hopefully."

The sand gave way to a stretch of rocky land, and there in the distance was the dark blue shimmer of the portal.

The channel to the Morningstar was still open a crack and the closer we got, the more the power writhed and thrummed.

"I feel something," Jilyana said. "It's through the portal."

"Another relic piece?" Asbeel asked.

"No." I stepped closer to the vortex. "Not another relic, but the being that they belong to."

Everyone gathered round, and Gabriel took my hand.

This was it. The moment of truth.

We stepped through the portal together. The world tipped, and when it righted itself, we were on stone floors surrounded by thick metal iron bars.

"Don't move!" A male in armor jabbed his spear at us through the bars.

Two others joined in, jabbing at us to keep us away.

No. No more. I was done. Rage born of exhaustion bubbled up inside me. "Enough! Back the fuck up. Now! Where is she? Where is Lucifer?"

The door at the far end of the room swung open, and Lucifer filled the frame, her chest heaving as if she'd run.

Her gaze settled on me and lit up in triumph. "Let them out. We have work to do."

CHAPTER 28

MICHAEL

The doors to the audience chamber open to admit me, and I feel the Dominion's presence before they speak. Their voice, their light no longer pains me because I too am filled with light, and I'm seething.

"Two days." My tone is clipped. "You made me wait two days for an audience when the information I have is vital to the—"

"We know about the conjunction."

They know? "Who told you?"

"You are not our only operative in the field."

They sound amused. How dare they sound amused? Maybe I should rethink standing down from taking over. Maybe they should be brought to heel.

"There is no need for you to worry, Michael," they say smoothly.

No need to worry? "Time is of the essence. If you know about the conjunction, then surely you agree we need to find a way to send sentinels through it. You say you've been searching for a way into Gehenna, a way to Lucifer for almost a decade, and now we have one. If we don't act, then Rue might find Lucifer first. You said we didn't need to worry about the relics if Shem was in our control, but things have changed now. If Rue has all the relics and gets them to Lucifer—"

"Enough!" The word is a reverberation. "We have given you power. Status. Some knowledge of our plan. But that does not give you permission to question us. We have processes in motion. If Rue does find her way to Lucifer, then it will be in our favor, and if she fails, then that too will be in our favor. There is no loss on the horizon for us, but for you...You can be stripped of the gifts we've given you."

Stripped? "You said I was restored, connected to the same font of power as you."

"Oh, Michael, did you honestly think we'd give you power that could not be taken away?"

Yes. Yes, I had. They'd tricked me. They'd fucking tricked me.

"You are blessed as long as we wish it, and as long as we continue to be blessed. If the Dominion falls, so do you. And not just a reduction of power, but true mortality."

They had me. They had me completely in their clutches.

"Now, Shem's body has been transported to the hub already, but we would like you to go there and prepare."

I want to argue, but I don't have any leverage. Not any longer. I take a breath and compose myself. "Prepare for what?"

"For our next arrival."

CHAPTER 29

RUE

Lucifer led us down a stone corridor, boots clipping against marble. Her sword sat in its holster across her back—an epic weapon with a jeweled hilt that seemed to exude power.

The air smelled of incense, a smoky, woodsy scent that was pleasant and should have been soothing, but the moths in my belly refused to calm.

We were here. Physically in Lucifer's fortress. We'd made it. So why did I feel so on edge?

It was the adrenaline of the past few hours still rushing through my veins, leaving me hyperalert and focused. Everything looked sharper and brighter. Even the gray light that filtered in through the windows glittered with motes of dust.

The walls were gray stone and hung with patterned tapestries, and despite the misty chill visible through the windows, it was warm and cozy inside.

"You made good time," Lucifer said, rounding a corner

to take us up a flight of worn stone steps. "I was worried you'd be felled in the outer circles. The eighth is especially brutal."

"We entered through the seventh," Gabriel said.

"The circle of souls. Thanatos's domain."

"We met him. He helped us."

"He's a decent sort. Visits from time to time but keeps his cards close to his chest." She shoved open the door at the top, and we were in the room from my dream. She moved quickly away from me as I entered, as if she was afraid I'd accidently touch her.

My scalp prickled. Something wasn't right here—more than her sudden aversion. Wait... "Why haven't you asked me for the relics?"

"I assume you have them." She drew her sword from its holster and propped it against a chair. "Why else would you be here?" She unbuckled the holster, shrugged it off, and rolled her shoulders.

"You *assume*? You can't *feel* them?"

Her mouth tightened. "Do you have them or not?"

Unease filtered through my veins. "Why can't you feel them?"

She made a sound of exasperation. "Because they were shielded from me by *him*. To prevent me from calling them to me and breaking our deal."

"God hid them from you?"

"Yes. He promised I would be made whole when I'd proven myself here."

"But he didn't tell you how, did he?" Gabriel said. "You don't know *how* to reforge the Morningstar, do you?"

"Reforge? I don't want to *reforge* it. I need to *destroy* it. I need to be whole. That's the only way I can help you. The only way I'll have the power to fight off the Dominion and reopen the gates to heaven. We *must* figure out how to destroy the pieces."

This couldn't be happening. "You don't know..."

She growled softly. "No. I do not know."

"But you told me...you..."

"I told you to bring them to me, which you have. Thank you. And now we will figure out how to release the power and make me whole."

Silence fell, thick and pregnant with disappointment. We'd come all this way...all this fucking way.

"And how long will it take to figure it out?" Gabriel asked.

She pressed her lips together and shrugged. "I...I don't know."

My limbs were suddenly heavy. My people were in danger. My world dying. I'd risked my life, and the life of the watchers to get the relics to her, and she didn't know how to use them?

I swallowed against the bitter tang in my throat and locked gazes with her. "I'm done here. I brought you the relics. You figure out what to do with them. We have to go back to our world...our people need us. Jilyana has a relic shard inside her. Draw it out and we can go." I held out my relic piece, and she shrank from it. "Why aren't you taking it?"

Her dark eyes gleamed with sorrow. "I can't. I can't touch it. Another condition. Another obstacle. He created a watcher to connect to the relic. One who was bound to it so that I would not be able to take it."

Shemyaza...

"It sounds like a punishment," Kabiel said. "Not a test."

Her left eye twitched. "His tests were always vicious," she said without bitterness. "It was his way." She turned her gaze on me. "But if that watcher is dead, then *you* are the only living connection to the Morningstar relic. You can help find a way to make me whole. I can't let you go. Not until we figure this out. But I swear to you, once I'm whole, I will use Soul Reaper to open a door back into your world." She indicated the sword propped up against the chair. "We'll leave together and stop the Dominion."

She'd withheld the truth, but she was still our only hope. What could we do but agree to—

"I'm sorry." Jilyana snatched the relic from me and stepped closer to Lucifer.

"Jilyana, what are you doing?" Asbeel demanded.

Her eyes were misty, but her jaw was set. "I don't have a choice. They have her. They have her, and I need to save her."

"What? Who?"

She grabbed Lucifer's arm, and the world behind her tore open, bleeding amber light that blinded us for a moment.

When it died, both Lucifer and Jilyana were gone.

And with them, the relics.

"What just happened?" Kokabel demanded. "What the fuck just happened?"

"Jilyana betrayed us," Asbeel said, his voice flat. "She lied to us. She was..." His voice cracked with emotion.

I closed my eyes for a beat. *Focus. Do not lose your shit. Think.* "The Dominion planned this. They must have let her go. They knew we were after the relics. They sent her to retrieve them."

"And to find Lucifer," Gabriel said. "Erelim was right. It was Lucifer they were searching for."

And they'd used Jilyana to do their dirty work. She'd

said she had to save someone. "I think they must have leverage on Jilyana."

"That doesn't make it right," Asbeel said.

"No, it doesn't, but I don't think she *wanted* to betray us." The woman I'd come to know the past few days wasn't a traitor. "I don't understand how she got Lucifer out of here."

"The Dominion have access to a power called the Word," Gabriel said. "It was something employed by the higher echelon. A way to extract celestial soldiers from danger. Some of us were given the power of a word. When uttered, it would pull us from wherever we were to a safe zone."

"So Jilyana has taken Lucifer and the relics straight to the Golden City?"

"No," Gabriel said. "I think they've taken her to their secret stronghold. They'll lock her down, lock away the relics."

"We have to stop them. We have to break her out."

"The location should be on the flash drive I gave to Bastian," Gabriel said.

"We can't do anything if we're stuck in Gehenna," Kabiel growled. "The portal we came through is gone. And even if we find one, could we even use it without a relic?"

But something that Lucifer had said rang in my mind. "Lucifer said she couldn't leave here. Not without being whole, which meant having the relic power back inside her body, right?"

"Right..."

"And she said once that was done, she'd use her sword to open a doorway back to our world."

"Where are you going with this?" Kabiel asked.

"What if the part of her that allows her to create doorways, any doorways, lies in the specific power of the Morningstar? Think about it. The Morningstar kept the fabric of worlds intact. It allowed us to walk through the conjunction, and its fracture caused doorways to open so... what if all we need to make a doorway is a connection to that power?"

"Which you still have!" Gabriel's chest heaved with pride. "Genius. It could work. Try it. Use the sword."

"Wait!" Kabiel grabbed my wrist before I could touch the sword. "What if it hurts you?"

"What if it doesn't? At this point, we've got to take the risk."

"Agreed," Gabriel said. "But I believe you're right, Rue. I believe this is our way out."

I took a deep breath and grabbed Soul Reaper by the hilt.

CHAPTER 30

BASTIAN

Bee sits by Tumiel's bedside, holding his hand. She's barely left his side the last three days.

Three days while we've been left cooling our heels with promises of a meeting with the general soon. Two days while the watchers and the reapers remain outside. The general of this base feels it would be too unsettling to the humans to have the watchers amongst them, despite what Mira and our party assert. At least I was able to get a look at the information on the flash drive. Schematics and floor plans and all sorts. A place called the hub. We have the location. It must be where the Dominion plan to hold Lucifer if they find her.

Bee looks up, sees me in the doorway, and quickly plasters a smile on her face, but her red-rimmed eyes tell a different story.

"How is he doing?"

"Stable. Healing. But the bullets did a lot of damage to vital organs, so...it's going to take a while, and there's no Rue to help speed things up..." She catches her bottom lip between her teeth and then slowly holds up his hand. The skin on his fingers is a darker red and his talons are longer and sharper than usual. "Bastian, I think...I think having to heal is using up his reserves of celestial energy and quickening his devolution."

Fuck. "Rue will be here soon. She'll be back, and she'll help. I know it."

"It's been five days since she left, Bastian. How long do we wait before taking action against the Golden City? Every day we wait means another day that the watchers devolve, and those that are already in devolution, the ones Rue helped, they'll lose themselves again and become a threat."

"I know."

"What do we do if she doesn't come back, Bastian?"

I hate this. Hate that this thought has gone through my mind more often than I'd like the last two days. "If Rue...If she's...lost, then so are the relics, and all we can do is make a home here." The words leave me empty.

"The watchers will be...they'll devolve. The reapers too."

"I know..."

She shook her head. "No. They have trained people here. Guns and we have a way into the Golden City. We can take it. We can take down the celestials."

"You're not thinking straight. There are hundreds of celestials. All of them are more juiced up than our watchers and can probably heal in a blink. We can't kill them with bullets, and trust me, we'd run out pretty soon if we tried. We can't risk exposing this last haven of hope."

"Agreed." A woman stands in the doorway, short blond hair slicked back from her forehead, cold pale eyes fixed on us. "I'm glad we're on the same page here." She smiles, but it doesn't reach her eyes. "I'm Lieutenant Storm. The general has asked to see you," she says to me before turning her attention to Bee. "Your...friend will be escorted off the base as soon as he's able to walk on his own steam."

Bee looks like she was about to argue, but then her shoulders droop. "Then I'll be leaving with him."

Storm's brows flick up slightly, the only indication that Bee's decision surprises her. "I thought these creatures were devolving."

"They are," Bee says. "But maybe having a reminder of humanity close by will help them hold on to themselves a little longer." Her gaze softens as she looks down on Tumiel. "Love is a powerful force, Lieutenant."

"You'll be permitted re-entry to the base once...when you need it," she says to Bee.

Bee looks up in surprise. "Thank you."

I follow Storm through the tunnels that remind me of the tunnels at the mall, except there are no devolved living here, just humans. As many humans as two of our regular bases.

The lieutenant says many were picked up a few weeks ago when the second wave of fractures spit a fresh wave of monsters into our world—aerial beasts able to get over our walls and bypass the runic security.

The count so far is eight hundred, and damn, does that figure sound good. But how long will it remain undetected by the celestials? If Rue fails, then how long before this base also falls?

Our worlds are bleeding into one another. How much time do we have?

"What is it like out there?" Storm asks.

"You don't know?"

"I wouldn't have asked if I knew."

"You've never been out there, have you?"

"No."

"Lucky for you."

She slows her pace so that she's walking beside me. "These watchers...celestials. They're friendly? You worked together and you weren't...afraid."

"Fear takes a back seat out there after a while. It becomes...normal. The watchers kept us safe. They kept us alive. They're my friends, and they're nothing like the Dominion or the celestials who follow their doctrine."

"And Gabriel?"

"What about him?"

"All I know is that he's been our contact for decades. I was a child when we came to this base, but I wasn't sworn in until a year ago when I made lieutenant. Only the uniforms know who Gabriel is."

"He's one of the good ones. One of the best."

She nods. "Good to know."

"But I wish you'd met Shem. He was..." I can't help but get choked up, and it takes me a moment to gather myself. "He was the true lynchpin. He sacrificed himself so that we could escape. If it wasn't for him, Rue and Gabriel wouldn't be in a position to go after the final piece of the relic."

"And this Lucifer? Can she be trusted?"

"I fucking hope so."

She stops outside a metal door with a plaque on it that says *General* and fixes her pale eyes on me. "You truly trust them, believe in them, don't you?"

I had my doubts to start with. "We've been through too much together for me not to know that I can trust them."

She gives me a curt nod, and then her cold, pale eyes warm. "I believe you." She pushes open the door and ushers me inside.

The room is snug and minimalistic with a desk, some

shelves, and a small seating area, along with some computer equipment and a whiteboard.

"Take a seat," she says.

"Where's the general?"

She rounds the desk and takes the seat opposite me. "You're looking at her."

CHAPTER 31

Storm is the general? "Why the subterfuge?"

"Not subterfuge, caution. Please sit."

I take the chair opposite her and wait for her to continue.

"We were warned by Gabriel that if he stopped contact, then he was compromised, and that we should move our base. He stopped communications almost two months ago. We were prepping to leave this place, and then you arrive. You have the code. You have humans. You have reapers and watchers with you. I needed to be sure that you weren't a trick sent by the Dominion."

That's why they didn't let the watchers and reapers in.

"Trust me, if the Dominion wanted to get into your base, they'd just blast their way in. They did that at the mall."

"Yes, well, now we know that. Now that I've had the chance to speak with your people and to observe you...I believe you are who you say you are."

"And now what?"

"Now we wait and hope that your friends return with

good news. But if they don't, then you have a home here. We could use a man with your skills."

I'll need to tell her how short my shelf life is, but that can wait. For now, it's enough that we have a place to stay. A home for all our people.

"Thank you."

"I've assigned you quarters, and your friend, Bee, once she's ready, will get her own also. But there's a spare room in yours she can bunk in for now if she wants. I understand that she was a scout at your previous base?"

"Yes."

"We could use her here. I'll fill you in on our security protocols and get you a pass for the computer labs. I'm sure you'd like to go over the schematics you found on your flash drive."

"That would be great."

She smiles warmly. "I'm glad you found us. Now let's hope that your friends find their way back from Gehenna soon too."

"BASTIAN, wake up. You're burning up. Hey!" Something cool kisses my forehead.

"Bee?"

"You have a fever."

"I'm fine. I'll be fine." My vision is blurry, heart racing, but it will pass…I hope.

Bee smooths the damp cloth over my face. "Is this…is it the serum?"

"Yeah. I'll be fine. It happens." I close my eyes. "It'll pass, and if it doesn't, then…then tell Rue that I love her."

"Shut up. You're going to be fine. And then you can tell her yourself when she gets here."

I hope. I wish. "I want to hold her one last time."

"You will." Bee squeezes my hand. "You fucking will."

I need to believe that. I need to hold on. The simmer in my blood ebbs then dies, and my heartbeat slows. "I'm okay." When I open my eyes, her face is clear.

"You fucking scared the life out of me," she says. "I heard you groaning and—"

An alarm blares, cutting off her words.

"What's that?" Bee demands.

"That means we have a breach."

ALARMS BLARE as we run toward the safe point on the far east of the base. Tumiel lies unconscious on his bed that has wheels, thank fuck. We've strapped him down so we can move fast. Still, the damn thing is difficult to maneuver.

"You're sure it's this way?" Bee asks.

"Positive." Storm showed me the spot earlier after she gave me a tour of the restricted areas of the base.

We hit a flight of steps that lead down to the safe bunker. A place built to withstand fire, flood, and hopefully celestial attack. It connects to an evacuation tunnel. One which the citizens have never had to use, but which Storm says will take them three miles away from this base and five miles from their next potential base.

Gabriel thought of everything, it seems.

Two uniformed guards stand at the door, ready to usher us inside.

I'm unstrapping Tumiel to haul him down the steps when someone calls my name from behind.

"Bastian!"

I freeze, my heart stalling for a moment before my pulse breaks into a gallop. Bee lets out a soft squeak, and I know...I know I'm not hearing things.

The alarms stop blaring as I slowly turn to look up the corridor.

Rue's hair is in disarray, her eyes bright in a face smudged with dirt, and is that the hilt of a sword sticking up over her shoulder?

"Hey..." Rue says. "Did you miss me?"

Her words are cocky, but the trembling of her mouth and the heaving of her chest tells me everything I need to know.

I bridge the distance between us, catching her as she throws herself at me. Her scent envelopes me, vanilla tones hidden beneath a bitter ozone smell. Her scent. This is her. And she's here.

She made it. And I'm never letting her go.

CHAPTER 32

RUE

The sword, which hummed with power a few hours ago was now silent and inert against my back. But it had worked when we'd needed it. I wasn't in on the metaphysical mechanics, but it reacted to the Morningstar power when I opened the channel, allowing me to will open a door back to our world. I'd imagined the forest near the church, and it had taken us there.

There'd been activity in the church.

Celestials.

Gabriel's hunch that the wards might fall had been right. We'd managed to sneak away undetected and gone on foot for a few hours before taking to the air.

We'd expected a warm welcome here. To find everyone inside the base safe and warm, but no, they had the watchers locked outside.

We'd used a second entrance to the base. One only Gabriel knew of and had access codes to. Still, alarms had been triggered, and I was certain we'd have been shot if the head of security hadn't been in the team come to counter us.

He knew Gabriel.

We were safe for now. I had Bastian with me again, and I'd managed to push some Morningstar power into Tumiel. He was with Bee, healing properly now. Although it had been harder to draw from the channel this time, as if it was resisting me, or as if someone was blocking it.

The Dominion must be doing something to the relic, which meant that time was running out.

There was no time for a proper reunion with Bastian and Bee before General Storm had me, Gabriel, and Bastian in her office, demanding answers.

The silence in the room was almost deafening once Gabriel finished briefing the general. She sat, chin tucked in, head bowed as if the weight of our failure was pressing down on her. She couldn't be much older than me, maybe mid to late twenties. But she had a weary look in her eyes. One that spoke of responsibility and burdens. Bastian stood by some shelves, his arms crossed almost defensively.

Oliver, the head of security, stood in the shadows behind Storm. Older, jaded. Silent. He watched.

Was he thinking the same thing as me? That the time for talking was over. That it was time for action.

"We must act now," Gabriel said, echoing my thoughts. "We must free Lucifer from the Dominion's grasp. She's our only hope."

Storm looked up at him, the beginnings of a sneer forming on her lips. "You said she doesn't know how to reclaim the power in the Morningstar relic."

Was she implying that Lucifer wasn't worth saving? It took everything I had not to step in and say something, but I clamped my mouth shut, allowing Gabriel to take the lead.

This was his forte. This was his base, and damn, did he look the part. Even with his auburn locks mussed and streaks of dirt on his face, the celestial radiated authority that was formidable to watch.

"We can figure out how to reclaim the power for her once she's free," he said firmly.

Storm made a soft mocking sound. "You want me to risk my people to free a celestial who might not be able to help us? You want me to send my men and women on a mission they may not return from based on a *maybe*?"

My hand itched to slap her.

"People have fought for less," Gabriel said coolly. "It's called hope."

She raised her chin, eyes glittering. "Not my people. Not our hope."

Was she serious right now? "Shemyaza sacrificed his life because he believed that we could fix this world. I went to hell because *I* believe we can fix it. And Lucifer believes she can too. All we need is a little time. If we can get her away from the Dominion, we can figure out the rest. Otherwise, how long do you think it'll be before the Dominion find you? How long before they take this base?"

"We've managed up until now," she said.

"Because of me," Gabriel snapped. He exhaled through his nose to rein in his emotions, and when he next spoke, his tone was cold and cutting. A tone I'd never heard from him before, one that both sent a shiver up my spine and excited me. "*I* kept you safe. *I* kept their eyes elsewhere, but I'm no longer there. I'm here, and there is nothing stopping them scouting this region. It won't be too long until they find you. You think you're safe? Think again."

She looked away, pressing her lips together.

My gaze went to Oliver, who'd taken a step forward then back again, as if rethinking his interference.

"Your father and I had a deal," Gabriel continued. "I gave him autonomy of this base. I gave him control, and he gave me his word that when the time came, he would fall under my command."

Her head whipped up, her eyes narrowing. "What are you saying?"

"I'm saying that this base belongs to me," Gabriel said bluntly. "I'm saying that Gregor was *my* second-in-command, and now so are you."

She pushed back her seat and stood, body vibrating with indignation. "You think you can *force* us to fight? Use us?"

"No," Gabriel said. "I can't *force* you. If you don't help us, then we'll do this without you. And once we win, once this world is free of the celestials, I can promise you that your people will not be welcome in the free cities. You can remain here, underground, hidden like the cowards you are."

"If I'm not mistaken, won't all celestials be pulled back to heaven when the balance is restored?" She arched a brow, her tone cocky. "Which means you won't be here to stop us."

Yeah, I didn't like this bitch. I didn't like her one bit. "You don't know that. None of us do. Lucifer could help make it so that some celestials stay. Maybe she'll restore the watchers and have them stay. You want to take the risk, then on your head be it."

She dropped her chin again. "You'd make all these people suffer because of my decision. How is that fair?"

"Fair? What fucking world do you live in? Life isn't fair, but maybe being tucked up down here, all safe and warm, means you've forgotten that."

"Your father knew better," Gabriel said, reminding me

that I was supposed to let him take the lead. I stepped back and snapped my mouth shut as Gabriel continued. "Gregor knew what was at stake and what needed to be done. We had an agreement."

Storm's throat worked for a moment. "Yes, well, he's dead, and the agreement died with him."

"Only because you choose to let it. Gregor was a good man. An honorable man. A courageous man who believed that this world could be saved. I'm sorry to see those qualities didn't pass to you." Gabriel turned to the door. "My people and I leave tomorrow evening. In the meantime, we'll be occupying the eastern sector of the base."

"What?" She leaned forward, fingertips pressed to the desk. "That sector is closed. Father said it was off-limits due to radioactive—"

Gabriel gave her a flat look.

She straightened, comprehension dawning on her features. "He lied."

"He told everyone what we agreed that he would. The east sector is for me and my soldiers. I have the codes to access it. If you decide to honor the agreement, you can send troops to join us there at 1700 tomorrow."

"You can't bring those monsters in here!" She rounded the desk toward us. "I won't allow it."

"I don't want to hurt any of your people, but if you attack mine, then we *will* retaliate."

"So much for wanting to protect humanity," she sneered.

I was so done with this bitch. "You have no idea what you're talking about, and if you sneer at him one more time, I'll slap your mouth off your face." I looked across at Oliver, still standing silently in the corner. "Well done on choosing a leader. You did fucking great. I bet your buddy is super proud right now."

Storm made a soft sound of indignation, but we were already exiting the room.

"Slap her mouth off her face?" Gabriel said, amused.

"Whatever. I was angry, okay?"

"Well, I'm flattered that you jumped to my defense. Those sneers she was throwing my way were beginning to get painful."

Bastian smiled. "Your face went all red."

I touched my hot cheeks. "I just don't get it. What is her real problem?"

"Whatever it is, I hope she reconsiders," Bastian said. "We could do with the numbers."

"I know," Gabriel said. "But just in case she doesn't, let's plan with the numbers we have. I'll get the watchers down into the eastern sector, you print out the schematics for the hub, and we can get to work on our extraction plan."

It was going to be a long night.

CHAPTER 33

The east sector of the base was huge, clearly designed to accommodate celestial-sized beings. The chairs had low backs to account for wings, and everything was larger to fit the celestial frames.

Gabriel had done this. He'd made sure his troops had somewhere to go if need be. The base went into the ground for several floors, and this sector was no different. Our watchers and reapers barely filled the space, highlighting how ill-equipped we were to go up against the Dominion and their vast army.

But what choice did we have?

"Here and here," Bastian said, pointing at spots on a schematic my brain struggled to make sense of. "Entry points that will probably be overlooked by security."

"Is that a sewer pipe?" Kabiel asked.

"Yes, about a quarter mile away from the hub. I pulled maps of the area off the database they have here. This pipe links to the hub. I doubt they even realize it."

"Okay, so we enter via the sewers?" Bee asked.

"Yes," Bastian said. "This here is where they'll be holding her."

"How do you know that?" Kabiel asked.

Gabriel placed his hands on the table and leaned in to study the plans better. "Because this is where all the power is being funneled to."

Bastian grinned across at him. "Exactly. It means that there'll be heavy security around it. Locked doors, scanners, sentinels, the works."

"Only authorized personnel will be able to get through," Gabriel said.

"We'll kill them all," Kabiel said.

"A lovely sentiment," Gabriel replied, "but the aim is to get to the hub undetected if possible."

I stared at the schematic, noting the many corridors and the huge chamber in the center. "How do we do that? How do we make sure we're not detected?"

"By creating a diversion," Gabriel said.

"Yes. Here, on the outside of the hub," Bastian replied. "We draw the celestials toward the attack. We hit them with such force that they're forced to push the majority of their resources toward the activity."

"We still have the problem of locked doors and scanners," Kabiel pointed out.

"I have a solution to that," Bastian said. "I can disable their systems. This room here is where the operating system of the hub is."

"Are you sure?" Gabriel asked.

"These lines here, and these boxes indicate the flow of power. Electrical lines and something else...Some other power source which leads to this structure on top of the building..."

"What is it?" Bee asked.

"I…I'm not sure. But it's built to hold this power… whatever it is."

"If you cut off the power in the operations room, will it cut off power to that thing?"

"Not sure. I'd have to take a closer look once I'm inside."

"It doesn't matter," Gabriel said. "As long as we can get into the central chamber, to Lucifer."

I had her sword, Soul Reaper. I had a feeling she was going to need it. The damn thing was formidable, able to cut a doorway in the fabric of a world and transport us home. It was a mighty weapon, and I was sure Lucifer would need it in her fight against the Dominion once we freed her.

"We need to organize teams," Bastian said. "Decoy team for the outside, and extraction team."

Just two? "What about you? You need a team to get into the security room."

"Not a team, maybe one or two people to keep watch. We need to be low-key."

"I'll come with you," Bee said.

"And me," Tumiel added.

He'd healed, but he still looked pale. I wasn't sure he was up to this mission, and from the look on Bee's face, neither was she. But I knew better than to question his fitness. Knew that he wasn't so arrogant as to come along if he felt he might end up being a liability.

Bastian must have surmised the same because he didn't protest. But Bee looked less than pleased, and even though she didn't question him openly now, I was certain they'd have words later.

"The extraction team should be small too," Gabriel said. "Grab Lucifer and head straight to the exit point."

"I'll lead the decoy team," Kabiel said.

Gabriel dropped him a nod. "I'll lead the extraction team. I'll take Rue with me. She has a connection to the Morningstar power, and we might be able to locate the relics along the way."

"Zaq and I will come with you," Sarq said.

"The diversion will draw some fire, but not all," Gabriel said. "They may even send more security toward their asset as protocol. We won't know until it happens. So we need a few more watchers with us to act as defense on the corridors closest to the holding chamber." He pointed at the two spots on the map.

"Four of my watchers," Kabiel said. "Two for each corridor. It's all we can offer without making the decoy team look like less of a threat." His silver eyes narrowed. "We have to hope they don't call in reinforcements from the Golden City."

"How far is the hub from the city?" Bee asked.

"Thirty miles," Erelim said. "But that's not far by air. Two decoy teams would have been better. One at the city and one at the hub. But our numbers are too low as it is. If we split them, we won't pose a threat."

"It's a shame I won't get to use my tunnel," Gabriel said. "It was guarded when we broke out, but the Dominion will have tripled the security, maybe even collapsed it by now. We still have allies in the city. We could have shaken the celestials to the core by attacking from the inside."

But Michael had put paid to that idea. The focus had to be on Lucifer anyway. "We can do this. We may not have the numbers, but we have the skill and the determination. We have a plan. We strike in the dead of night, and we take back the power."

"Get some rest," Gabriel said to everyone. "Find a bunk and sleep. Fuel up tomorrow and be ready to move at sunset."

The next few hours would either fly by or drag. Either way, I doubted I'd be getting any sleep.

CHAPTER 34

Hot food was bliss, and we all ate in silence, huddled in small groups. Bee and I were joined by Sarq, Tumiel, Zaq, and Mira. The reapers joined Baraqel and his watchers, while Kabiel and his watchers took their food and retreated to the lower level. Gabriel and Bastian were still poring over the plans, but I'd set aside some food for them both.

The stew was meaty, which meant they had access to cattle. Probably a farm close by, or even below ground. From what Gabriel told me about the base on our journey here, it was built to be fully equipped to sustain life for many decades to come.

"Shem would be so proud to see you now," Sarq said, pulling me out of my thoughts. "He always knew you were a survivor."

"We had our doubts to start with," Tumiel said. "But you proved us wrong a long time ago."

"Having you with us is like having a part of him with us," Zaq said.

I'd held thoughts of Shem at bay to keep myself from

crumbling, but memories, soft and tender, filled my head now, and my heart bloomed with the sweet ache of loss.

I blinked back tears. "Nothing feels the same without him. This mission...this purpose, it's all that keeps me going, and once we do this...once we fix this, then what? You'll be gone. All of you." My vision blurred. "And Bastian..." I looked across the room at him leaning over the table, his face a map of concentration. "I don't know how long I'll get to keep him." I dropped my gaze and took a breath. "I don't want to lose you guys. You're all I have left. You're my family."

Bee took my hand and squeezed, and I saw my fears reflected in her eyes. What if she didn't make it either? In that case, I didn't want to survive. If everyone I loved was gone, then what was the point?

Sarq exhaled heavily. "This world has become my home now, and you're a part of that. I swear it, Rue. If there is a way for us to stay, then we will." He looked at Tumiel and Zaq. "We all have reasons to want to stay now, after all."

Mira leaned against Zaq, and he put his arm around her. She'd joined us a little while ago after bawling out the guards who tried to keep her away. She'd entered with all the others yesterday, only because Zaq had insisted, but now he was here, there was no way she was leaving his side unless she had no choice.

"I wish I could go with you," she said now. "I wish I could help."

"You help by being here," Zaq said. "You're my person to come back to. My person to stay on this world for."

"Maybe Lucifer will be able to help with that once she's free," Bee said hopefully.

It was all we could do. Hope.

Hope that we'd survive tomorrow night.

Hope that Lucifer would be able to fix our world.

Yeah, a lot was riding on hope's shoulders.

THERE WAS a communal washroom in the east sector, a long room with an open shower area as well as some smaller stalls. I showered quickly, wanting the grime of the journey gone, then dressed in fresh clothes secured by Mira, who was already making connections among the human population here.

Tomorrow night would test us all, and I needed to make sure that the watchers were fueled up. With Shem gone, I was their only connection to the Morningstar power, but I suspected my connection might be cut off soon. The Dominion were up to something with the relic pieces, and my gut told me I needed to make as much use of the power as I could now.

I started with Sarq, Tumiel, and Zaq, then moved on to Baraqel and his watchers. I worked in batches, having them hold my hand, my arms, and my wrists while I opened the channel for a minute or two at a time. The power didn't rush out like before, but the steady stream was still enough.

Once everyone on the upper floor was fueled, I headed to the lower floor where Kabiel and the devolved watchers had set up camp.

I went to Kabiel first, but he shook his head. "Do the others. I'll wait."

"My connection is weakening; I'm worried I might not be able to channel much by the time I get to you."

"Then I'll be fine," he said. "The others need it more."

"We'll wait too," Asbeel said, glancing toward Kokabel, Yomiel, and Matarel.

I worked in batches again, and each time I channeled, it got harder. By the time I got to Asbeel, Kokabel, Yomiel, and Matarel, the power was a thin stream, but I held the channel open for three whole minutes, pushing as much into them as I could.

Finally, it was Kabiel's turn. He drew me away from everyone and into a small room set aside from the main bunk chamber.

I reached up to cup his face, my go-to when it came to him, but he gently grasped my wrists before I could make contact.

"You're exhausted," he said. "I can wait a few hours."

I shook my head. "You don't understand. I may not be able to access the power by then." He smiled wryly. He knew? "Kabiel, you need to be fueled. You're leading a team, and you were expending so much energy in Gehenna. We need you, and I'm not willing to risk you devolving now."

He sighed and released me, allowing me to press my palms to his cheeks. His eyes fluttered closed as I opened the channel and let the Morningstar power out.

It trickled, weak and barely there. I needed more. *Come on.* A slight surge of power, then the thin stream again. Not good enough.

He opened his eyes and gripped my wrists again. "It's all right, Rue. I'll be—"

"Kiss me."

"What?"

"Just do it and make it good."

His brow arched. "Good?"

Shem had fed his watchers residual power through his connection to the one relic piece he'd managed to keep hold of until he'd found me—a human housing the piece of his soul that had a direct connection to the Morningstar power.

I was a channel, and there was one thing that always heightened the power.

Arousal.

The Dominion had the relics and Lucifer. I doubted they'd be keeping an eye out for spikes in Morningstar power now.

"Make me feel...something."

His chest rumbled, and a shiver ran up my spine. "Something." His hand slipped from my wrist to my throat, curling around my neck in a callused caress, and my breath caught. If I closed my eyes now, I'd imagine it was Shem touching me.

"Do it," Kabiel said. "Let me give you that much in exchange."

He guessed what I was thinking, and shame heated my cheeks.

I searched his face, noting the dull almost flatness to his eyes. I wouldn't use him like that. "Shem is gone, and I don't need you to keep the memory of him fresh in my mind. His every word, every breath is etched into my heart."

A soft glimmer filled his eyes. "To have felt that...To have had it...Can I...Can I pretend I have it with you...just for one moment?"

A fist claimed my heart. "Yes. Just for a moment."

His grip on my throat flexed as he drew me close. My mouth parted on a gasp, and he claimed it, crushing his lips to mine, his free arm wrapping around my waist while he forced me into an arch. His hand around my throat flexed, cutting off my breath then releasing it, leaving me lightheaded yet grounded as he tasted me with deep, rough strokes. For a moment, I forgot the reason for the kiss, able to do nothing but clutch at his shirt as heat rushed up my body.

Need.

Want.

Power.

I opened the channel, and it rushed out to meet him.

He groaned into my mouth, and my pussy throbbed.

No. I didn't want this. Not now. Not with him. I tore my mouth free, cutting off the connection to him and to the power.

He held me for several beats before allowing his hand to slip from my throat and his arm to unwind from around my waist.

"Thank you." His tone was rough.

I didn't look at him. I couldn't.

My heart hurt, guilt and shame clawing at me. "I...I have to go."

He didn't stop me as I hurried from the room and back to the upper floor.

I needed to wipe that kiss from my mind. I needed to wipe the memory from my body.

I needed Bastian.

CHAPTER 35

BASTIAN

Rue rushes into the room that I've claimed for us. Her cheeks are flushed, her eyes bright, and my stomach turns because I know that look.

It's her afterglow.

"Rue, what happened?"

She closes the door and presses her back to it. "I asked Kabiel to kiss me."

I'm instantly on the defensive before my brain computes that she went to channel power. "You were fueling him?"

"Yeah, but...Bastian." She squeezes her eyes shut. "I asked him to make me feel something. I needed to feel arousal to channel because the Morningstar power is being blocked." She gives me a pleading look, as if she's afraid I won't believe her.

"Rue, it's okay." I cup her shoulders. "It's okay."

She shakes her head. "No. It isn't because I felt...It felt good. I wanted him. For a moment, I wanted him. And in Gehenna, Gabriel and I shared a bed, and it...it felt good. I wanted to be close to him." She covers her face. "What is wrong with me?"

My heart sinks because sharing her with Shem was hard enough, but if Kabiel and Gabriel are putting her emotions into knots like this, then it means they might become just as important to her in time.

Time...My time is running out, and once I'm gone, I don't want her riddled with guilt every time she feels close to another male. I don't want her shutting down her emotions. I don't want her to go unloved.

I gently pull her hands away from her face. "Hey, look at me. Rue...Look at me." She finally lifts her chin. There are tears in her eyes and my heart hurts to see her like this. Torn up and in turmoil. "Shem and I agreed to love you how you needed to be loved. To give you the freedom to choose. Although in Shem's case, that freedom would come with his seal of approval of course."

She smiles wistfully. "Yeah, sounds like Shem. You guys spoke about this stuff?"

"Once." I tucked a tendril of dark silken hair behind her ear. "We talked at length once. We agreed that we wanted you safe and loved and secure no matter what. Gabriel is a decent celestial, and from what Shem told me, Kabiel was his right-hand man. An honorable watcher. When all this is said and done, if they stay, you shouldn't run away from your feelings."

She searches my face. "I'm not ready. I don't think I'll ever be ready to give my heart to anyone ever again." She strokes my jaw lightly with her fingertips. "After Jamie, I didn't think I could feel again, but you and Shem, you brought me back to life. You made my heart thunder. But the roar in that thunder died with Shem, and once you're gone..." Her mouth trembles, eyes welling. "Once you're gone, this heart will be dead."

"Then you find someone to bring it back to life. You hear me? Promise me."

She shakes her head, dislodging tears.

"Dammit, Rue." Impotent anger floods my blood. Rage against fate that plans to take me from her too soon. I crush my lips to hers, hands sliding into her hair and fisting to hold her to me. She sobs into my mouth before falling into the kiss.

Her back hits the door, and there's suddenly a frenzy in my blood to be near her, to be inside her, connected in the most primal way.

I need her naked. I need her beneath me. I need to show her...make her feel. It takes mere moments to strip off her clothes and carry her to the bed and another moment to tear off my shirt and shuck off my pants. She stares at me, chest heaving, rosy nipples begging for my kisses. The bed is small, but we won't need much room with me on top of her.

I'm like a beast hungry for her flesh, lapping and sucking, teeth grazing every sensitive spot until all I can hear are her pants and her whimpers. Her scent spikes, drawing me to her core, and I devour her, barely feeling the rake of her fingernails as she grips my hair, holding me to her core and urging me not to stop with each breathless cry.

Her body shudders with release again and again, her sweet nectar coating my tongue. I wait until she goes limp before lifting my head.

She looks down her body at me with heavy-lidded eyes, her mouth still parted. She licks her lips, and my cock jumps, sweet pain tightening the small of my back.

"Bastian...please." She draws me up to claim my mouth and reaches between us to grip my cock. "Please."

I'm not about to deny her the very thing my body is screaming for.

I enter her with a deep thrust that rocks her body. Her eyes pop wide before fluttering closed.

"Oh...Oh, please..."

I cup her delicate jaw with one hand and claim her mouth before pulling out of her, slow and easy.

She makes a sound of protest in her throat, and I punish her by nipping her bottom lip.

She digs her nails into my bicep. "Fuck me."

I slam into her, eyes rolling back at how fucking slick and tight she is. I want to be controlled. I want this to last, but my body takes over, each thrust harder, faster, deeper, until it feels like my cock is inside an undulating velvet vise.

She comes again, body going stiff as the orgasm rocks through her. I manage two more thrusts before I join her in oblivion.

THIRST PULLS ME FROM SLEEP. Rue snores softly in my arms, and for a moment I consider ignoring my thirst. But my throat feels dry, and my body screams at me to get some water.

I carefully roll her away from me, slip my arm from beneath her, and wait to make sure she doesn't stir before pulling on my clothes and heading into the communal area.

There are a few watchers dotted about. Sarq and Penemue, Baraqel and one of the devolved watchers who went to Gehenna with Rue, but the kitchen is empty. I don't bother to switch on the lights; there's enough light coming in from the communal area to illuminate my path to the sink.

I pour a large glass of water and down it in three gulps. My hand trembles as I set it down, and I grab my wrist to calm the involuntary spasm.

"How bad is it?" Gabriel says from the doorway.

"It's getting worse." I shake my hand, but the tremor lasts for several seconds more.

He steps into the room with a sigh. "I have to ask...Are you up to the mission?"

I hold out my now steady hand. "Yes. They don't last long."

"Does Rue know about them?"

"No. And she doesn't need to. Not yet."

I refill the glass and drain it.

"Thirst is another symptom," Gabriel says, his voice tainted with sorrow.

"I figured."

"How is Rue? She looked upset when she came back from seeing Kabiel. I spoke to him, but he was...evasive."

"She's fine, just...Look, Gabriel, you and I don't know each other too well, but Shem trusted you, and Rue...well, you guys have a bond, so—"

"We broke that bond in Gehenna," he says flatly. "I died for a moment. Rue brought me back." His mouth slants in a smile. "That woman is something special."

The look in his eyes isn't one of lust, it's fondness. It's... love. The green-eyed beast inside me stirs, but I slap it down. "She'll be broken once I'm gone. She's lost so much. I need you to promise me that you'll do everything in your power to make sure she doesn't lose you."

His eyes flare in surprise. "I promised Shem I would protect her and—"

"I'm not talking about protecting her, although that's important too. No. I'm talking about love."

"Rue and I aren't in love."

"The road to love looks different for everyone, and sometimes those on it don't see it for what it is. But those on the sidelines...we have more of a perspective."

He dropped his gaze. "I care for her, more than...more than I have for anyone in...forever."

"Then I need you to fight to stay with her once this is over. You, the watchers, and Kabiel."

He arches a brow. "Kabiel?"

"Rue is a woman with deep feelings. Fiercely loyal to those she gives her heart to, and that heart will need mending. Healing. Nurturing. I need you to promise me you'll be there to do that when...when I'm gone."

He considers for several moments before replying. "I promise."

I like him. I like the fact that he doesn't try to give me false platitudes, telling me that it will be okay. That they'll find a cure for me. I appreciate that.

"Thank you."

A sense of peace settles over me in knowing that no matter what tomorrow brings, Rue will be looked after, and when she feels that her heart is dead, there'll be someone to bring it back to life.

No matter what tomorrow brings, I can walk into it in peace.

CHAPTER 36

STORM

I've lived underground all my life, but for some reason, today, I long for a window to the outside world. Even the sunroom, a chamber designed to provide our bodies with the necessary vitamins, doesn't lift my mood. Not even looking at the landscape through our hidden cameras helps.

The itch to run free, to feel a real breeze on my face, to touch the earth outside gnaws at me.

My quarters feel like a cage—too small and constrictive—and the conversation with the celestial circles my mind like a vicious vulture.

"What happened to the alpha team wasn't your fault," Oliver says. "We took a risk because we needed to. It's what your father would have done." He looks perfectly relaxed lounging on the sofa, ankle resting on his knee, but I know his tell—the bobbing of that knee—he's on edge.

I meet his gaze with a steady one of my own. "We lost twenty men and women because of that one risk. Twenty humans lost is twenty too many. We're going extinct, Oliver. I need to keep us alive."

"There'll be no life if the Dominion win. Gabriel is right, they'll find us, and when they do, we'll be prisoners living to serve them. You know what happens to humans in the Golden City."

Yes. Yes, I know. Father hadn't kept that information a secret from us here at the base. He believed we needed to know what was at stake. If he hadn't gotten sick…If he hadn't died…

"He believed you'd make a good leader," Oliver says. "And so do I. You've done a fine job, and I've had no quarrel with any of your decisions up until now."

Ouch. That hurts. But honestly, who am I kidding? My gut is in knots with conflict, with doubts, and this man…this beautiful man who's managed to get under my skin and into my heart, knows it.

He knows me. "Our people are no match for the celestials. They'll merely be a diversion. Cannon fodder."

"And you know that the celestials will do their best to avoid killing any humans," he points out. "We're too valuable to them."

The knots in my stomach spawn more knots, leaving me nauseous. "You're not going to let this go, are you?"

"No. I believe that our troops should be given a choice."

"So that I can absolve my guilt?"

"No, so they don't blame you for keeping freedom out of their grasp."

Fuck. This role…This responsibility feels suddenly too big. "You should have been general not me. I should be working under you, not the other way around."

The corner of his mouth tips up. "There is one place you

can work under me, *and* on top of me." He rises and moves toward me. "Any position you like..."

My blood heats, and I reach up to loop my arms around his neck. "I'd like that."

He brushes his lips against mine once, then again, this time with a little more pressure. My pulse spikes in anticipation, but he pulls away, his pupils dark and hungry.

"I love you, Lila, and everything is going to be okay."

I need to hear it, even if it might not be true. "Come on, let's go give our people a choice."

CHAPTER 37

SHEM

Michael's sapphire eyes blaze with triumph as his blade pierces my heart.

My heart.

Rue.

I'm sorry.

A wave of dark sorrow washes over me because I'll never see her again. Never hold her again. *Please don't break, my love. Don't let this destroy you. You're stronger than this.*

Michael orders his men to retreat as darkness grips me.

I'm dying.

But it's all right.

I allow my eyes to drift closed, falling willingly into the arms of oblivion.

Again.

How many times have I relived this moment? Is this death, now that heaven is closed? This endless loop of devastation?

Michael's sapphire eyes blaze with triumph as his blade pierces my heart, and once again sorrow grips me. The same thoughts, the same grief and emptiness.

This isn't real, not anymore, and I'm ready to move on from it.

Michael vanishes, taking the pain that pierces my body with him, and I'm alone, floating above a misty world with a blanket of stars above me. The silence holds anticipation, as if it's waiting for something.

What now?

Where do I go from here?

I'm dead, and where do dead celestials go now that there is no heaven for our consciousnesses to return to?

Maybe I can stay. Watch over Rue from the other side? A ghost. I can be a ghost. As soon as I think it, I'm flying. Not with my wings, no. There's no need for those.

I fly above the world, over forests and roads until I spy the church far below me. It's wreathed in light, glowing softly like a beacon. If I had a heart that could beat, it would hammer at the sight of all the twisted shadows that surround the place.

The dead.

The dead are here, lingering on the outskirts of the light as if it's a campfire that can warm them, and I instinctively understand that there is no getting through the barrier. Not for them, and not for me.

Something tugs at my chest, insistent and strong, and in the next moment I'm being dragged away from the church and into darkness.

A bubble of panic swells in my chest because this is bad. This force that has me in its grip must be fought, but I'm a powerless shadow now, with no fight left in me. I don't want to go where this pull is dragging me, but I have no choice.

"Ah, there you are," a female voice says. "I thought I sensed you close by."

The hold on me slackens, the knots in my chest ease, and warm arms wrap themselves around me. The scent of sulfur fills my head for a moment, and in the next instant, I'm standing on my feet in a room lined with books. A fire crackles in a hearth bracketed by two armchairs, and a tall regal woman stands beside one of those chairs.

Why do I feel as if I know her? We've never met.

"It's good to meet you, Shemyaza," she says.

"What is this place? Who are you?"

"This is merely a construct. A pocket of reality which the Dominion cannot breach."

The Dominion? She knows of them, and she has power. Enough to pull my essence to this place. "Who are you?"

"My name is Lucifer, and I need your help."

Lucifer is a myth. A story told to celestials to keep them in line…isn't it? But this being…I know her, I feel her power, and it's familiar. It feels like home.

"Yes, Shemyaza. I am home. I am the Morningstar."

It makes sense now. Her power runs through me also.

"I thought your essence out of reach when your human told me that you were dead."

My human? "Rue? You saw Rue?"

"Yes, and now that I see you, now that I feel you, I know that you are not dead. You are in the Dominion's grasp, just as I am."

Hope floods me in a gentle wave of heat. I'm not dead. My essence is still grounded, trapped by the Dominion, and Rue…Rue found a way to speak to Lucifer? My beautiful, clever Rue. She's out there somewhere, and I'm not dead. I need to wake up. I need to break free!

"Yes," Lucifer says. "You must wake up, Shemyaza,

because now that you're here, I finally understand what must be done to free the human world, and my dear watcher, *you* are the key."

CHAPTER 38

RUE

Dawn came too soon, and the day passed quickly in preparation for our departure that evening. The hub was thirty miles east of base zero. The sentinels and Powers may have even flown over this location several times. The base was lucky to have remained undetected. We had an hour's worth of flying ahead of us and then...then the plan.

The extraction.

My appetite died even though I felt like there was a pit in my belly. I found a quiet spot at the kitchen table where I could polish Soul Reaper's hilt in peace. The gem embedded in it gleamed in the artificial light.

"You should eat something." Gabriel joined me and placed a bowl of pasta in front of me.

The smell made me want to puke. "I'll be sick if I eat."

"You'll be sick if you don't." He claimed the seat beside me and gently took my hands, stalling my obsessive polishing. "Put the sword down and look at me."

I did as he asked, allowing myself to meet his eyes, allowing him to see my emotions—fear, doubt, and more fear. "People are going to die tonight."

"Yes. There will be deaths." He held my hands, his grip firm and reassuring despite his words. "This is war, Rue. No matter how fast we are, how stealthy we are, there will be deaths on both sides. But the world will live. This world, your world, will finally breathe again. "

I swallowed to moisten my throat. "I hate that I'm scared, not of the fight, or of getting to Lucifer, but of losing people. My friends and family. People I love...you..." He blinked sharply. Surprised. A soft laugh rode my exhale. "Like you don't know."

"Don't know?"

"That I care about you. You're my friend and...more... There could be more one day, I just—"

"You don't have to explain yourself. This connection we have is undeniable, but it needs time to breathe. We can give that time if you want. We can see what it becomes. Once this is over."

"If you stay..."

"I'll do everything in my power to stay, Rue. I swear it." He stroked the backs of my hands with his thumbs. "There is nowhere in the cosmos that I'd rather be than by your side."

Butterflies filled my chest. "I think...I think Shem and you would have been good friends."

"I know we would have." He let go of my hands and reached for the bowl of pasta. "And he'd tell you to eat."

Maybe I could eat a little, because the smell of the food no longer made me want to puke.

BASTIAN HELPED me into Lucifer's holster. I was smaller than the celestial, and the damn thing was an awkward fit, but we managed to get it to sit snugly on me. Bee claimed my bat as a weapon, and Tumiel spent ages fussing over a holster he'd made for it, ensuring it didn't cut into her.

Then it was time to leave.

We headed topside but were blocked off in the corridor by Storm and her security guy. They weren't alone. They had several uniformed men and women with them.

A troop.

My gut tightened, but Gabriel stepped forward, his posture relaxed and unthreatening.

"Is there a problem, General?" he asked.

"Yes, there is," she said. "You're not going anywhere...Not without backup."

My shoulders sagged. Thank fuck.

"What changed your mind?" Gabriel asked.

"The people." Her gaze flicked from Oliver to the troop behind her. "I gave them a choice, and they've chosen to accompany you."

It looked like we'd be able to give the celestials a little more of a challenge.

The decoy team just got larger.

I FLEW WITH GABRIEL, my body wrapped around his, my face tucked against his neck so I could feast on his scent. His heart beat a steady rhythm, and mine fell into pace with it.

We were hurtling toward danger. I should have been terrified, but there was something about Gabriel that soothed that part of me.

"We're almost at the landing point," Gabriel said.

Shit. Okay, now I was nervous.

We dropped altitude, and my insides twisted into knots. I took a steadying breath. We could do this. Everything would be all right.

It had to be.

Shem's sacrifice wouldn't be for nothing.

The churning inside me stilled as Gabriel's boots met the earth. He hugged me to him for a moment before relaxing his grip.

"We're here."

Here was in a heavily wooded area with a field ahead of us, and beyond that was the hub. Another mile out.

The sewer access was close by and would take us under the building and into it.

The others landed around us, and the hum of engines approached as Storm's troops joined us. They'd driven the vehicles that Bastian had found.

Kabiel alighted with Bastian a moment later, followed by Bee and Tumiel, Sarq and Zaq, Baraqel and Penemue. Everyone was here.

"Kabiel, wait thirty minutes after we're in the sewers, then head for the hub," Gabriel said.

Kabiel nodded.

"I'll set a timer," one of Storm's men said. "You have the radio?"

"I have mine," Bastian said.

"I have the other." Sarq held up his radio.

"Good," the man said. "The radios are set to the same channel. You'll call in when you've disabled the security so the extraction team knows they can go in. The extraction team will radio once they have the cargo and are back in the tunnels. Decoy team will remain active until then."

Everyone had their instructions. It was time to go. I looked over at Kabiel and gave him a nod. "Be safe."

He smiled, but it didn't meet his eyes. "Always."

The knowledge that I might never see some of these faces again left me hollow, but I pushed away the feeling and straightened my spine.

We had a job to do. "Let's move out."

CHAPTER 39

The pipes leading to the hub hadn't been used in some time, but the smell was still awful. Thank goodness my olfactory system stopped registering it after a while. We moved fast and silently. Everyone focused on the task ahead.

Bastian and Zaq took the lead—the scout in Zaq having memorized the network of tunnels on the plans we had. Tumiel and Bee were a little behind us, and behind them were Sarq, Asbeel, Kokabel, and two others I didn't know.

We climbed a flight of metal steps onto a walkway that led to a steel door.

"Through here," Zaq said. "It'll take us into a basement that leads up into the hub."

Bastian yanked open the door into a small cylindrical room with pipes built into the wall either side of a series of metal rungs leading to a large grate in the ceiling.

"Basement access," Bastian said.

Our gazes locked, and my lungs grew tight.

"I'll go first," Gabriel said.

He moved fast to get to the grate and then shoved it open

with a snap of metal and a scrape of rust. He didn't look back before leaping out, and my heart hammered against my ribcage, the urge to call out to him an itch in my throat.

His face appeared in the aperture above. "All clear. Come up."

Bastian ushered me up, following close behind.

The basement was damp and smelled of mildew, weak moonlight filtering in from a tiny window high up toward the ceiling.

"This was part of the old building," Bastian whispered. "But according to the plans, it still connects to the hub. There's a storage space, then the main building."

"Kabiel will be storming the main entrance any minute," Bee said.

"Good." Gabriel led the way up the stone steps to the basement door. "We'll wait till the security alarms go off." He tested the door. "Locked." He twisted hard and pulled. The door gave. His eyes gleamed in the gloom. "Not anymore."

We didn't have long to wait before a shrill ringing beat against the basement door.

Gabriel gave a nod then threw the door wide. The alarm blared loudly as we filled the storage room.

Gabriel beelined for the main door and peered out into the corridor. "It's clear." He closed the door and turned to Bastian. "We go right?"

"Yes. Zaq knows the way. The security room is left and up a floor."

We waited a few more seconds as the alarm continued to blare. If anyone had been on this side of the building, they would have had time to rush toward the main entrance by now. Anyone that was left we'd have to deal with.

This was it.

This was the moment.

Bastian's team would go first. They had to shut down the security systems, so...

My gaze tangled with Bastian's to find my turmoil reflected back at me. He pulled me in for a hug, resting his cheek on my head. "I'll see you afterwards. I love you." He pulled away enough to cup my face and press his lips to mine. "I love you so much."

"I love you too. Be safe. Please."

"I will. I promise."

I turned to Bee and hugged her too. "No heroics."

"Same to you." She gave me a squeeze.

Gabriel stepped away from the door, pulling me back against his chest. I leaned into him, my eyes burning as Bastian turned to the exit.

He looked back one more time, the corner of his eyes crinkling in a smile.

Then he was gone.

I took a shuddering breath. "Fuck."

"They'll be okay," Gabriel said. "We can do this."

I had to believe it. "How long do we wait?"

"Five minutes and we head to the next storage room along the way and wait for him to radio," Zaq said.

Gabriel continued to hold me, and I gripped his arms, fingers flexing against his taut muscles as I counted down the seconds.

"We should go now." Zaq cracked open the door. "Clear."

We were on the move, but I wouldn't relax until I heard Bastian's voice on the radio.

CHAPTER 40

MICHAEL

There is nothing but blessed silence in the viewing room above our prize. This chamber is built to keep out sound. In this space, all is peaceful. All is power.

The Dominion have outdone themselves. My doubts have evaporated because they've succeeded where I now know I would have failed.

The vast room below me—the central chamber of our hub—glows with ethereal light from the energy of four relics and their anchor, each connected to the one being who can save us all.

Lucifer floats above the ground, her head tipped back, eyes white and sightless, body shimmering with power where the energy from the relics connects to her. Five connections passing through her and a sixth shooting out, up into the roof to feed the machine that will convert it into raw, pure, celestial power.

Enough power to fuel an army of celestials. Enough power to allow the higher echelon on this earth to never go hungry again, and the lower celestials...well, they'll still have the humans to feed on.

Yes, we will nurture the humans. Feed them. Free them of disease so that they can contribute to the new order. This new engine of life.

Never will heaven rule us again.

I was wrong about the Dominion. They had a plan, and that plan is coming to fruition today, and tomorrow... Tomorrow I will satisfy my heart's desire and conquer the thorn that plagues it.

Rue will need a protector. I will be it. I will bring her home.

The door to the viewing room opens, and a sentinel enters. "Supracelestia, we have a problem."

"There are no problems, only solutions."

"Yes, of course. But the hub is under attack. Watchers and humans."

I arch a brow. "It is? How novel. Kill them all."

"Even the humans?"

"If need be."

"Very well. Some have breached the building." He hands me a small screen which shows security footage of sector G of the facility.

My pulse leaps at the sight of the woman on screen.

"I've dispatched sentinels to intercept them."

"No. Call them off."

"Superacelestia?"

I give him a flat look. "Do not make me repeat myself."

He bows and quickly exits, and I turn my attention back to the screen. Back to the small team who've managed to get inside our hub. Gabriel, always the strategist, but not today... Today he fails. Today he dies. But not her.

Not Rue.

She's come for Lucifer, but she's headed straight for me.

CHAPTER 41

BASTIAN

The route to the security room is clear, and foreboding simmers in my stomach. I quash it and set my mind to the task in front of me. What kind of security protocols will I have to disable? In my life before the fall, I'd built things, tinkered with technology and computer programs, but after two decades of being without any decent kind of hardware or software, I'm rusty.

Still, I can't fail.

I doubt the celestials will have top-of-the-line stuff. At least, I hope they don't. We hit the stairwell leading to the security floor, and with the alarms blaring, it is impossible to hear if anyone is headed down toward us from an upper level.

But once again, we make it up the stairs and onto the first floor without incident. The lights here are dim and tinged red, the alarm much louder, so it makes it harder to think.

I grit my teeth and hurry toward the security room. No

celestials block our path, and my foreboding grows, but then we are at a door blocking off the corridor to the security room, and my gaze lifts to the symbol above it.

The warning for radiation.

"I know that symbol," Bee says. "We learned it in scout training." Her eyes go wide. "Radiation."

The figures beneath the symbol explain how much radiation, and my stomach drops.

"Oh..." Bee covers her mouth. "That dose...that's lethal."

She's right. The amount of radiation beyond this door will be lethal without the proper gear.

"We need to find the proper clothing," Bee says.

I look to Tumiel and see my hunch written all over his face. There won't be any gear. "Celestials aren't affected by radiation, are they?"

"No," Tumiel says. "Which means the signs are for the benefit of humans. To warn them not to venture farther. The Dominions obviously plan to bring humans to work here at some point soon."

"Then what do we do?" Bee asks.

"I can go," Tumiel says. "Bastian can tell me what to do."

If only it was that simple. "I won't know what to do until I get into the room and into their systems." A strange calm comes over me as the inevitable conclusion settles in my mind. "It has to be me."

"What?" Bee looks from me to Tumiel, then back again. "No. You'll die if you go inside."

I give her a wry smile, ignoring the yawning pit inside me that's already mourning the loss of what little time I have left. "I'm already dying, and there's no time for arguments. This has to be done, and I'm the only one who can do it."

Her eyes well. "Bastian..."

Yeah, she knows it, and so does Tumiel. He stands hands fisted, jaw tight with rage.

"Hey, when this is over, when the world is back to rights, make sure my soul gets to where it needs to be, would you?"

Tumiel's eyes well, and he exhales sharply before pulling me in for a hug. "I will find you, my friend. I swear it." His tone is thick with emotion, and my heart squeezes painfully in my chest.

I break the hug, only to be enveloped in another by Bee. "I'm sorry," she sobs. "So sorry."

"It's all right. This is good. This is better. No more waiting and wondering when. I get to go out a hero." She sobs harder. "Tell Rue...Tell her I love her. Tell her...tell her goodbye." I pull away from her and tug my tools from my pocket to set to work on the numeric security panel. "Go. Get to the central chamber and rendezvous with Rue."

Bee shakes her head and reaches for me again, but I look to Tumiel. "Take her. Please. Go." I need to do this alone before I lose my nerve.

He takes Bee's hand, his eyes filled with sorrow. "Goodbye, friend."

I turn back to the panel, not wanting to see them leave.

Focus, Bastian. We're on a fucking clock here in more ways than one.

It doesn't take long to bypass the lock. I take a deep breath, shut out the terror, and shove open the doors.

The room is bathed in red light, darker than the corridor. I move fast toward the back room and into a space filled with machines and huge cylindrical cannisters marked with the radioactive symbol. A network of pipes connects them all, and suddenly it all makes sense.

This is their fuel.

This place is powered by radioactive material.

I need to shut it down.

My head swims as I park my ass at the control panel and work on accessing the system. It doesn't take long. The system is basic.

My stomach aches, and a wave of nausea washes over me. I start going through the shutdown protocols one by one. There are so many. Layers and layers. The fuel powers everything. This intricate, lethal machine is one huge bomb waiting to be detonated.

And maybe that's exactly what it is. Maybe this is their insurance policy against us. Bile shoots up my throat, and I swallow it down, blinking against the sharp pain in my head.

A tremor fills my body, and I grit my teeth and continue hitting keys until the last piston has been shut down.

The alarms die, and silence allows me to hear the rush of blood in my head.

It's done.

I'm done.

I tug the radio from my pocket, fighting the tremor in my limbs, and depress the button.

CHAPTER 42

RUE

Something was wrong. Something bad. "It's been too long. Something must have gone wrong."

"It's fine," Gabriel said. "Bastian will radio us any—"

The alarm stopped, leaving us in heavy silence, which was broken a moment later by static followed by Bastian's voice. "All clear. Over."

Gabriel lifted the radio to his lips. "Great work, Bastian. Now get to the sewers. Over."

"Will do. Over."

My scalp pricked. He sounded odd. I grabbed the radio off Gabriel and pushed the button. "Bastian? Are you okay? Over."

"I'm fine. Go. Save Lucifer. I'll see you soon. I love you. Over."

But my gut was telling me something was off. "Bastian? Are you hurt? Bastian, where's Bee? Over."

Static followed and then silence.

"Something's not right. We have to go find him."

"There's no time," Gabriel said. "Rue, we have to save Lucifer."

"You sense it too. You know something is off."

He gripped my shoulders. "We have a mission. People are depending on us. Rue, the decoy team won't last forever."

Every atom of my being wanted to break away from him and run toward the security room, to Bastian.

"Shem died for this, and Bastian..." Gabriel inhaled through his nose, his expression stoic. "If something *has* happened, you need to make his sacrifice worthwhile."

Something had happened, I knew it with every fiber of my being, just as I knew I had to keep going. Had to move forward against the gnawing pain inside me. I swallowed a sob.

"We can't let Michael and the Dominion win," Zaq said.

I was surrounded by watchers willing to risk their lives. There was no room for selfishness, not now. Not here.

"Let's move."

IF BASTIAN WAS HURT, then we'd fix him. He'd be fine. Tumiel and Bee were with him. Everything would be okay.

The sooner we got Lucifer and got out of here, the better.

Asbeel, Kokabel, and the other two watchers peeled off from our group, stopping at the intersections that led to the central chamber.

No one stopped us. No sentinels attacked. The decoy was working, but it wouldn't work for long. We had to move fast.

Zaq took the lead with Sarq. Gabriel and I followed close behind. He held my hand in a reassuring grip, channeling that same soothing aura that he seemed to exude.

Yes, everything would be fine.

The corridor became a tunnel that led to a single metal door with a keypad lock. If Bastian had disabled the security, then the door would open without a code. Zaq grabbed the handle and tugged.

The door opened with a soft hiss.

My body broke out into gooseflesh. There was power beyond this door. "Lucifer. I feel her."

"Then let's get her," Zaq said.

We filed into a room filled with light. Light that streamed from the center of the room where Lucifer was suspended midair. Light coming from the relics and... Jilyana...The djinn was tied to a post, light pouring out of her abdomen, eyes white and unseeing, and beside her was another figure—large and crimson, wings folded tight, head bowed.

My heart stopped for a beat then broke into a gallop. "Shem!" I rushed toward him, but a figure landed in my path.

Gold-tipped wings flared, catching the light, glowing so brightly I had to throw my arm up to shield my eyes.

The light dimmed after a moment to reveal Michael, chin tipped up, looking down his nose at us imperiously.

"Rue, so nice to see you again."

I craned to look past him to Shem, unconscious but alive. He was alive, and he was here, and my heart felt as if it would burst. "What have you done to him?"

Michael's lip curled in disgust. "Nothing, despite my best efforts. Apparently, Shemyaza can't be killed by a celestial sword. But he serves a purpose here. A handy anchor to help channel the relic power back to its source."

"You plan to use Lucifer's power to fuel the celestials," Gabriel said. "You want to use her as a battery."

Oh, fuck...

"We can, and we will. Shutting down the security systems has no effect on how this room works."

Because this room was powered by the relics. By Lucifer herself... "The huge orb on top of the building...that's where the power is going, isn't it?"

"Ah, Rue, you are so smart. So perfect. Come here." He held out his hand, beckoning me. "Come to me, and I'll make sure you live. I'll protect you, and in time, maybe we can arrange for you to visit Shemyaza."

He was serious? He actually believed I'd join him. "Fuck you, Michael."

His eyes darkened. "You will respect me!" His voice echoed around us, a terrifying boom of authority. "Come here now!"

Gabriel stepped in front of me, wings flaring, and Zaq and Sarq joined him, creating a barrier between him and me. "You want her, you'll have to go through us."

Michael's eyes lit up as he smiled widely. "Gladly."

He threw out his hands, and twin streams of power shot out and slammed into Gabriel sending him flying backward.

My cry was cut off by Sarq's and Zaq's bellows of rage as they charged at Michael. I ran to Gabriel, my heart in my throat.

He clutched his blackened chest. "Wake Lucifer." He pulled himself to his feet and joined the attack on Michael.

Three on one should have been a breeze, but Michael looked unfazed. He batted at them, laughing. He was playing with them. Their power was no match for his.

We needed Lucifer and Shem.

I rushed into the center of the chamber, into the light surrounding her. "Lucifer!" I grabbed her legs and pulled, but the force that had her in its grip refused to let up. "Wake up, you have to—"

A loud shockwave hit me, flinging me away from Lucifer and onto the floor. Soul Reaper dug into my back painfully, and I rolled onto my front, scrambling to stand.

Gabriel, Sarq, and Zaq were on the ground across the chamber from me. Unmoving.

Michael strode toward me, a dark look on his face. "Enough! You come with me. Now!"

I reached over my shoulder and gripped the hilt of Lucifer's blade. A rush of power coursed down my arm as the sword that had been inert since leaving Gehenna surged to life.

I drew it from its holster and stepped away from Michael. "Stay back."

His gaze flicked from the sword to me, then a mocking smile curled his lips. "Holding a sword is very different to wielding one."

My stomach trembled. "I trained as a sweeper before I was a scout. I know how to wield a fucking sword."

He reached over his shoulder and drew his glowing weapon. "Let's find out, shall we?"

"Rue!" Gabriel ran toward us.

Michael flicked his wrist, ejecting power that knocked Gabriel off his feet, sending him flying back to hit the wall. He struggled to be free but was held by an unseen force. Zaq and Sarq met the same fate.

Michael was too powerful. There was no beating him. No winning this. But even as my hope died, determination rose to take its place. I'd fight him. I'd force him to expend his energy, and with his focus on me, maybe...maybe the others would be able to break free.

He twirled his sword, circling me. "Go on, Rue, attack me."

"No. You want me. Come and get me."

His eyes lit up in a smile that said he thought this was some cute game. The Michael I knew was gone, and this creature standing before me was corrupted by power. Insane from it.

He ducked his head and rushed toward me, sword arching in a swing.

CHAPTER 43

SHEM

Each corridor, each turn, takes me closer to the surface, toward consciousness. Each moment unfurls my essence from the special hiding place I didn't know I possessed. I'm almost ready to slip back into my skin. Almost ready to be whole when the corridor ahead of me blazes bright.

"There you are," the Dominion's voice booms around me. "We've been waiting for you."

Pain lances through my head, taking me to my knees.

"You think you can escape us? Outwit us? There is no escape for you, Shem. Go back to your hidey hole and sleep. There is no place for you in our new world."

Sleep? Why were they asking me to sleep? Why not just kill me?

Because they can't. They can't do anything, Shem. Lucifer's voice is a whisper in my mind. *When have they ever done anything themselves?*

And it all suddenly makes perfect sense, and if by magic the pain in my head is gone. I slowly pull myself to my feet.

"No. What are you doing? Get down. Get back on your knees."

My lips smile for the first time in what feels like an age. "Make me."

The light blazes brighter and a frisson of fear rushes up my spine, a primal instinct related not to them, but to God. To *his* divine wrath, to *his* power. Not the Dominions.

Never the Dominions.

They can't hurt me. They can't hurt anyone without someone else to wield their sword.

I duck my head and break into a sprint straight into the light.

CHAPTER 44

RUE

Michael rushed me and I tensed, ready to evade, ready for the dance that would keep him occupied. My mind screamed at me that this was insane, that there was no way to beat him, but Soul Reaper hummed in my hand, funneling conviction into me.

Michael's sword arched toward me, and I brought Soul Reaper up on instinct to counter.

The clang of metal on metal, the hiss of power, a shockwave of impact up my arm, a flash of light, and I swung away from him, giving in to muscle memory and allowing the sword to lead me.

Because it was.

It was driving me.

Another clang. Another impact. I cried out in pain at the shockwave that rocked my muscles.

My body wasn't equipped for this.

Michael stepped back, shoulders heaving. "You are truly

formidable, Rue. I cannot wait to have you writhing beneath me. To taste you. To own you."

What? No. No way. "That's never going to happen."

But Gabriel and the watchers were still pinned, screaming words that I couldn't hear from behind a shield that Michael had created.

I was alone.

I was tired.

And the power in the sword was burning through my body. An involuntary cry fell from my lips.

"Drop the sword," Michael said. "Before it damages you too much." He frowned in concern. "Rue, please, drop it. It doesn't have to be this way. Just come with me. I can heal you."

"I'd rather the sword kill me than be with you."

His expression shuttered. "Then so be it." He swung at me, and this time I knew it would be a killing blow. Knew that I wouldn't be able to counter, even as the sword brought my arm up to do so.

A primal roar shattered my eardrums, and Michael was knocked off his feet by a crimson blur.

Shem!

He was awake. He was fucking awake, with his fist pummeling into Michael's face over and over.

The blade in my hand glowed brightly, and Shem's voice filled my head. *"The relics, Rue. Use the sword to destroy the relics. It will free Lucifer. Hurry, I won't be able to hold him off much longer."*

I turned and ran toward the nearest relic shard and swung the sword at it. The blade connected with a thunderous crack, and the fragment disintegrated, cutting off that stream of light. No time to stop. I hit the second fragment, then the third, aware of Michael's yell of rage and Shem's counter bellow.

There was only one relic left.

Jilyana.

Her eyes were no longer white.

She was awake, trapped but conscious, the relic glowing inside her chest like a beacon.

"Please..." she begged. "Save her. Save my daughter."

Daughter? She had a child? That's how the Dominion had controlled her? It made sense. My will faltered, and her expression hardened.

"Do it, Rue. You have to do it. It's the only way to stop them and save us all. I know that now. I'm sorry, so sorry for not having faith before. For believing their lies."

"Rue, hurry up," Shem cried in my mind.

Fuck. "I'll find her. I'll find your child. I swear it."

I struck hard and fast, piercing her body and shattering the relic.

She exploded into embers, and the final stream of light went out.

"No!" Michael cried.

I spun in time to see Shem palm-punch him in the chest to send him flying across the chamber.

Gabriel, Sarq, and Zaq hit the ground as an echoing voice filled the chamber—not one voice but many speaking together.

"You will not fall Michael. You are one with us. You are the Dominion."

Michael rose to his feet, his body glowing with inner light that lit up his golden hair so it looked like embers of the sun had been woven into each strand. His sapphire eyes blazed like blue fire as they raked over us.

"You will all fall!" His voice reverberated around us, pure power. Lethal and irrevocable.

We were screwed.

To my left, Lucifer's voice filled the chamber. "My sword!"

Soul Reaper yanked itself free from my grip and shot across the room to land in Lucifer's hand.

She stood tall and commanding, hair flying about her face in a phantom breeze, eyes like twin stars blazing with wrath.

Michael's gaze whipped toward her, and the fire in his eyes dimmed. "No..."

"Yes." Lucifer advanced.

"No." This time Michael's voice was not his own. "You will not win. We will not allow it."

Michael's arm came up, sword arching toward Lucifer and stopped, midair. "No..." Michael whispered. He dropped to his knees and tipped his head up to look at her in a dawning comprehension that I didn't understand. Tears streamed down his cheeks.

I wasn't sure what was happening here, and I didn't care. I had Shem back, and that was all that mattered.

I rushed toward him, and he gathered me to him, crushing his lips to mine in a kiss that was filled with the aching throb of no more tomorrows.

No, this was wrong. He was back. He was mine. I clutched him to me, fingers digging into his biceps, his shoulders, because I knew...somehow, I knew that once this kiss ended, he would be taken from me. I channeled every unsaid emotion into that kiss, every ounce of love and longing as my heart slowly shattered.

"Shemyaza, we must hurry," Lucifer said. "More

celestials are coming. I must ascend now. I cannot save this world otherwise."

Shem broke our kiss and briefly pressed his forehead to mine. "I love you, Rue, with every fiber of my being. Nothing and no one can take that from you."

Michael's mouth parted and his irises went white. "No. You must not. You cannot," the Dominion cried.

Oh...fuck. Michael was fighting them. He was fucking fighting them, and Shem was trying to pull away from me.

I gripped him tighter, but he broke free and crossed to Lucifer. She held out her sword to him, which he took and flipped, pressing the tip of the blade to his chest.

Suddenly it all made sense. My foreboding, the sense of impending doom and loss. Everything.

He was the key.

The anchor.

Lucifer couldn't be free while he existed, and that sword...That sword would end him for good.

Movement above us and around us signaled the arrival of more celestials.

"Now, Shemyaza!" Lucifer said. "It must be now."

But she was wrong. It wouldn't be enough. Because a piece of his soul existed intertwined with mine. And there was only one true way for her to be whole.

A calm conviction settled over me.

This was always how it was meant to be.

Shem plunged the sword into his chest, and I threw myself against his back.

My body jerked as the blade sliced into me, burning, tearing as it pierced and bound us together.

"NO!" Gabriel's heart-wrenching scream was followed by several bellows of shock.

But it was okay.

Shem was in my arms.

"Rue..." Shem's voice was a rasp. "Oh...my Rue..."

"I'm here, Shem." I laid my cheek against his back. "Always and forever."

The world exploded with warm light as we tumbled into oblivion together, because God had never meant this proud brave watcher to die alone.

EPILOGUE

Death isn't the end.

I mean, I knew that, but with Soul Reaper doing the ending, I kinda thought I'd be obliterated.

But nothing ever truly dies; at least that's what I've been told.

Ascension, for Lucifer, meant something much more than I'd realized.

It meant taking God's place.

All the power.

The right to rule.

Lucifer took it all because she was God's heir.

I'd like to say I was there to see it unfold. That I was there when she kicked the Dominion's ass and obliterated Michael. Damn I would have liked to see that. But I was on a journey of my own.

An ascension of my own.

You see, the soul has its own voyage, and my soul...well, it wasn't as new as I'd been led to believe, and when I was in that in-between state, not completely obliterated, but not grounded either, everything made sense. The knowledge of the cosmos was mine. But that time that felt like a blissful eternity ended too soon.

"Ah, there you are, little one. Open your eyes." Lucifer's voice coaxed me back to being.

I emerged from the endless light to find her looking down at me. Where was I? What had happened?

I'd died.

Shem too...

Where was Bastian? Gabriel? Where was—

"Hush now. You're safe. Everyone is safe."

I sat up on a bed in a decadently decorated room, all cream and silver and filled with afternoon sunlight.

"Where am I?"

"Home." Lucifer smiled.

She was no longer dressed in her battle clothes but was in a loose-fitting shirt and dark slacks. Her hair was braided, the tail dangling over her shoulder, and why was she looking at me with such wonder?

"Where is home...exactly?"

"Heaven, Rue. This is heaven."

"I died."

"Yes. Your mortal body is gone, and your soul was revealed in all its glory."

"I'm confused. How am I here?"

"Because this is where you belong, Rue, just like me. You see, gods procreate by either sharing their divine essence with another god or by creating a being from their own essence. The god of this world did the latter. Twice. Once with me, and then again with you."

"Wait...what?"

"Yes, Rue. God is our father, and you and I...we are sisters."

THIS WAS INSANE. It was totally impossible, so why was there a calm inside me? A gentle acceptance as if...as if I'd known it all along. "I was mortal."

"Your test was mortality. Your test was fixing that particular world, just as mine was managing Gehenna. Our father loves tests just as much as he loves creating beings from the ether that connect us all. We are both here now because our tests are complete. He promised me ascension, and I have it, but I believe he sent you into the world blind."

"Yes, I...I don't remember him. I don't remember my creation. But the Cherub we met a while back said I was created specifically to house a piece of Shem's soul."

"Your mortal body was, yes," Lucifer said.

An awful thought occurred to me. "Wait, what about Shem? Was he...Is he our brother?"

Her eyes twinkled. "No, Rue. Shem was created by our father and Thanatos in a collaborative effort. He was the anchor to the Morningstar relic which housed a piece of my soul. You see, you and I have both been fractured. You on earth and me in Gehenna. I'm whole now, and so are you. When Soul Reaper ended your body, the fragment of your soul that had been on the mortal realm reunited with the divine aspect of you. You know this, you feel it. But it will take time for it all to assimilate."

She was right. I did feel it. I felt connected in a way I'd only ever felt with the watchers. "The Dominion?"

Her mouth thinned. "Gone. Their essence dissimilated and thrown back into the ether. They were created without form. Never blessed with the ability to create their own physical bodies. Their power lay only in their control over the scribes and the reputation they built here before the fall."

"And Michael? He tried to fight them in the end."

"Yes, he did. We spoke and he realized his mistake. Maybe I would have forgiven him, but he was tainted by ambition and greed, and I fear in time he would have made the same mistake again. Some souls crave power, and Michael is one of them. I could not suffer him to live. He was also dissimilated."

Michael had made his choices and his end was fitting. But the others? "What about Shem, Gabriel, and Bastian? What about the watchers, and Bee? Are they okay?"

"You know that Shem was obliterated by Soul Reaper, but you may not know that your friend Bastian also perished."

I'd known, deep down, I'd known as soon as he'd hung up the radio. My eyes heated, but I blinked back tears because if she was now the new God here and I was her sister then... "We have to bring them back."

The corner of her mouth lifted. "I thought you might say that." She stood and held out her hand. "Come with me."

I allowed her to lead me from the room, out onto a balcony that floated above mist. Steps came off that balcony extending up into clouds and more mist to join with other balconies where disembodied doors waited.

"This is heaven?"

"The central hub of heaven. Every nodule of heaven can be accessed from here. You'll get used to it."

Because I was staying here? But what about earth? The people? My friends? And there was something else. A promise I'd made. Jilyana's face filled my mind. "The djinn, Jilyana, she said she had a daughter. I believe the Dominion were keeping her hostage to control Jilyana."

"Yes." Lucifer sighed. "There was indeed a child, born of a celestial and djinn union. An abomination that the Dominion kept hidden until she perished."

"What? She's dead?"

"A long time ago, but they didn't tell Jilyana that. I saw it all in their collective memory when I ended them."

All this time they used her. They lied to her. Poor Jilyana. "She didn't deserve what happened to her. "

"No, she did not. But let us turn our thoughts to happier things." She led me up a stairwell suspended over nothing and through a door into a cozy living room, and my worries melted away at the sight of the occupants.

Two celestials, with glowing white and gold wings, broke off their conversation and turned their attention to me. My heart skipped several beats. Because I knew these faces. Shem's features were etched into my memory, except now he'd been restored, bronze and beautiful, chestnut hair laced with gold and neon blue eyes piercing my soul. And Bastian...Bastian looked larger and exuded radiance.

Lucifer had ascended him somehow. Made him a celestial.

"A gift, dear sister," Lucifer said. "I'll leave you to your reunion."

She slipped away, and I ran to my guys. They cocooned me in a group hug and showered me with kisses as they wrapped their wings around me.

"This is a dream."

"No, Rue, this is reality," Shem said. "Forever." He cupped my face and kissed my forehead.

"Look at you." I beamed up at them both. "You look amazing."

"You should see yourself," Bastian said. "I didn't think you could get any more beautiful than you already are."

My cheeks warmed. "The others? Are they all right?"

"Yes. They're on earth," Bastian said. "We've been rebuilding. Gabriel dismantled the Golden City and tore down the walls. The watchers have been cleaning up the surrounding areas of any monsters that weren't sucked back into Gehenna. Bee's taken a leadership role in the city too, and Storm is helping."

"The world is healing," Shem said.

How long had I been gone? It didn't matter. I was here now. "I'd like to see it. I…I want to see everyone."

Shem stroked my cheek. "Gabriel should have been here too."

"I told him to come," Bastian said.

I swallowed the lump in my throat. "Why didn't he?"

"I don't think he feels it's his place," Shem said. "Not yet anyway. But you can change that, Rue." My gaze shot up to meet his and he smiled. "It's all right to let your heart love him."

"He's a good guy," Bastian said.

"Yes…yes he is." I looked from Bastian to Shem. "Please, take me home."

TWO MONTHS LATER

New Hope City stretched out below me as far as the eye could see. The view from the Freedom Tower was impressive, proving how much could change, how much could be accomplished by the will of the people.

The monsters were gone.

Gehenna was sealed once more, and humanity was beginning to thrive. The people had a new government headed by the leaders who had kept the majority safe in their time of need. Storm, Oliver, Bee, Mira, and several others had come together to create a council and form a new democracy, where the people who'd had their voice taken away were given it back.

My watchers and I had helped, but our work here was done.

It was almost time to leave.

"Hey?" Bee said joining me on the pinnacle. "Gabriel said I'd find you up here."

"It's beautiful, isn't it?"

She came to stand beside me. "It is. It truly is." She sighed. "Do you have to go?"

This place, which had once felt like home, was beginning to feel more and more alien to me as time passed. I was changing, becoming whole, becoming who I was meant to be, and that being didn't belong on this world.

Still, I'd miss the people. I smiled and turned to face her. "I will come visit, and one day...one day you'll be with me." I looked up at the sky. "Up there."

"You best make sure I get a decent view."

"You know I will. No matter what, you and I...we'll always be friends."

She pulled me into a hug, and I breathed her in, sweet and slightly sweaty and wholly human. Unlike me.

She broke the hug and reached up to push my hair out of my face. "How soon after the ball do you have to leave?"

"At dawn."

Her gaze flicked over my shoulder to my wings, and I folded them tighter against my back. They were a beautiful silver which shimmered blue in certain light, but I was still growing into them. They felt too large, too elaborate, unless I was flying. Then...then they felt just right. I hadn't quite gotten the hang of hiding them yet, but Gabriel said that skill would come with time.

"What do you think Lucifer has planned for you all?"

"I don't know."

Nerves fluttered in my belly because my sister had been cryptic in her message asking me and Gabriel to return to heaven. Gabriel and I were the only celestials left in the city. The other watchers had returned a week ago.

Kabiel and his scouts had been the first to be summoned back. Kabiel, fully restored, had a sharp beauty that never failed to pierce my heart. But he'd kept his distance, and I was grateful for it, because there was the threat of something there that I wasn't ready for.

Baraqel and his team were summoned next, and finally Shem, Bastian, and Sarq. Tumiel and Zaq had been given leave to stay here in the city as representatives of heaven, and a direct line to Lucifer should the humans ever need one.

"Did you try on the dress I had made for you?" Bee asked. "Did it fit?"

I hadn't had a chance to. "Not yet. But I'm sure it will be fine."

"I made sure there was space for your wings."

"I'm sure it's perfect. And you? Is Tumiel escorting you?"

She blushed. "He is. He...he asked me to marry him."

My heart leapt for her. "That's wonderful!"

"Mira and Zaq are getting married too."

A regular human marriage, not the twisted bonding that the Dominion had forced on the humans. There would be no more procreation between celestials and humans. The Nephilim had been called to heaven where Lucifer had assigned them celestial roles.

"Is Gabriel escorting you?" Bee asked, a sly look in her eyes.

It was my turn to blush. "Yes."

"Have you two..."

"Not yet."

"Why not?" She sounded genuinely curious, and honestly, I didn't have a proper reason.

"I don't...The timing is...Urgh. He hasn't tried. I mean, I know he wants me, but he's so...gentlemanly."

"Then maybe it's time you take the initiative and jump his bones. Look, he probably doesn't want to push you. He's giving you time and space, but if you're ready, you need to let him know."

"By jumping *his* bones?"

She grinned cheekily. "Pretty much."

Maybe she had a point. The past two weeks, with the others gone, Gabriel and I had gotten close, real close, and the sexual tension was killing me.

"I'm going to do it."

"Good!" Bee kissed me on the cheek. "Right, I've got to dash. Last minute prep before the big event tonight."

She headed to the lift that would carry her down the tower, but I had a different route in mind. And a specific destination.

I climbed up onto the balcony, spread my wings, and stepped off.

I LANDED on the balcony to Gabriel's quarters and instantly doubted my eagerness. What if I'd read the signs wrong? What if he wasn't into me that way? Shit, this was a bad idea.

I turned away, ready to leap back into the sky.

"Rue?"

Fuck. I plastered a smile on my face, formulating a viable reason why I'd be snooping on his balcony and turned to face him, but the words shriveled up and died on my lips at the sight of his naked torso, all gleaming and cobbled and begging to be touched. My gaze traveled down, as if drawn by unholy forces, down to the waistband of his tantalizingly low pants and—

"Rue, my face is up here."

I looked up quickly, cheeks burning. "I am so, so, sorry. I was just...just..."

"Admiring the view?" He arched a brow. "Is that why you came, Rue? To look?" He ambled closer, and the tension that was ever at the ready between us spiked. "Or did you plan on sampling?"

I was locked in his emerald gaze, breath trapped in my throat. "I want...I want...you."

"About fucking time." He bridged the rest of the distance between us and scooped me off my feet. "You, my beautiful celestial, have been an exercise in restraint." He carried me into his room and carefully laid me on the bed with my wings spread out beneath me.

But he didn't join me. Instead, he busied himself with closing the drapes and lighting candles.

I pushed up onto my elbows. "What are you doing?"

"Setting the mood." His eyes were dark with hunger as they connected with mine before flicking back to the candelabra. "I want our first time to be special."

"We don't need candles for this to be special, Gabriel. It'll be special no matter what because it's with you."

He swallowed hard, his chest heaving, then crossed the room to join me on the bed. He stretched out beside me and propped his head on his hand to look down at me. "Why did you come to see me, Rue? Truly?"

"To tell you that I'm ready, that if you want me, then I'm ready, and that...that I fucking want you so bad it hurts."

He traced my jaw with a fingertip, trailing it down my throat, over my collarbones, and stopping just above my breasts.

My breath hitched. I wanted him to continue. To touch me. "Gabriel, will you make love to me?"

"Yes, Rue, with fucking pleasure."

He planted kisses along my jaw until he reached the sensitive spot just below my ear where he parted his lips and softly sucked on my skin.

Pleasure rolled down my body, nerves tightening at my breasts and between my thighs. "Gabriel..." My voice was breathless as he whisper-kissed his way to my mouth, and when his lips finally claimed mine, heat rushed up to meet my skin, sensitizing every inch of my flesh so that every brush of his fingers, every stroke of his tongue lit a fresh fire of need inside me.

My wings stretched and pulled at my back as he gripped my wrists and tugged my hands above my head. The sensation, a sweet pain, seemed to connect to my pussy, leaving me with an aching throb that needed assuaging.

He covered my body with his but didn't settle his weight on me, allowing pockets of warm air to spread out between us and slip beneath my clothes to caress my suddenly fevered skin.

I needed to feel him. Naked and slick against me. Inside me.

But he held me captive, plundering my mouth, devouring me with kisses that left me whimpering and begging for more.

GABRIEL

I don't want to rush this. I've waited for so long. Yearned for this connection, this admission, and now that I have her pliant and ready beneath me, I don't want it to end, despite the ache in my loins and the burning need to consummate.

She tastes like nectar. Her lips, soft and pillowy, her tongue—fuck, I could suck on it all day. But I move down to her breasts, straining against the confines of her shirt. Yes, that needs to come off.

I don't mean to tear it, but fuck, it's done now. Oh heavens, she feels so good in my hands, so sweet in my mouth. Every gasp, every cry, inflames me more, and I taste her, every delicious inch, as she writhes and begs, pushing up her hips as I get closer to the epicenter of her need. I can smell her desire, and my mouth pools with saliva.

This time I'm careful, peeling her slacks down past her hips to expose the fruit of her desire. My fruit now.

I free her of her clothing, part her slowly, then dip my mouth to her. Her juices coat my tongue as I taste her, alternating between long, leisurely strokes and feathered laps. She swells and melts against my lips, bucking and grasping at my hair.

Yes. This is mine. Mine. Slick and swollen, just for me. I push my tongue inside her, and she grips it and squeezes.

"Gabriel, please." Her voice is a strangled plea.

She's ready, and so am I.

I sit back and push down my waistband to free my arousal, and her eyes go wide, stroking my ego in a way that makes me harder and larger.

"Give it to me," she demands.

There's a growl to her tone, hungry and primal, and the

compulsion to satisfy rushes over me, something only a celestial female can accomplish.

Something that, with a severe lack of females in heaven, has been a sensation long missed.

I revel in it now, eager to give her what she demands. She's wet and warm, stretching to accommodate me but oh so tight. I have to slow down, ease in, inch by inch, until blood is pounding in my head and the nerves at the base of my spine are bunched so tightly I'm afraid I'll find my release before I can enjoy hers.

I seat myself, and we both groan in unison. Our gazes connect, and she sucks in a breath as I pull out slowly, then gasps as I fill her again. I settle into a rhythm, slow and easy, deeper and deeper, and her walls grow tighter—pulsing, begging me for more. But I need her to say it. I want to hear it.

"Please, Gabriel. I need it. I need it hard."

"What do you need?" I ease out and thrust once more.

She bares her teeth. "Fuck me. Fuck me until I can't breathe."

RUE

My demand lit up Gabriel's eyes. He grabbed my hips and flipped me onto my front. My wings flared, then spread flat across my back, tips reaching for the edges of the bed. He cupped my ass, tilting me before entering me with the sweet stretch that burned a path to my heart.

Each thrust hit home, bringing me closer to the release I craved.

"Yes. Yes."

The wet slapping sounds we made served only to heighten my pleasure.

"Fuck," Gabriel said. "Fuck, Rue, you're so fucking tight. I need...Fuck..." He growled, his hips a piston against my ass.

A surge of heat rushed up to hug my throat, and my vision whited out as I came over and over with every thrust.

He made a guttural sound and stilled, grinding his hips against me as he filled me with his heat.

He leaned over me, still pulsing inside me, his hands roving over my wings, stroking the muscles that tethered them to my back and sending fresh shivers through me.

He kissed my nape. "I love you, Rue."

Tears filled my eyes. "I love you too, Gabriel."

MY DRESS WAS a deep iridescent blue that spilled around my frame like a magical waterfall and made my wings stand out. The deep V cut a path between my breasts almost to my navel, but it was cut to hug, to fit. I had no idea who Bee had commissioned to make the dress, no idea where the gorgeous material had come from, but it felt wonderful to feel pretty for once.

"You should put your hair up." Gabriel appeared in the mirror behind me. "You have a beautiful neck."

I turned to him, taking in his midnight blue suit, fitted to accentuate his broad shoulders, slender hips, and powerful thighs. His wings were hidden.

"I need to learn to hide my wings like you do."

"They're still there," he said. "Just on a slightly different plane. It's called a shift. I'll teach you once we're back in heaven." He raked me over slowly. "You truly are beautiful, Rue."

My stomach fluttered. "And so are you."

He stepped closer and cupped my nape, pulling me in for a soft kiss that plucked at my lips, leaving me breathless. "If you don't stop, we might not leave this room."

He ran his hand up my side and cupped my breast. "Don't tempt me."

I arched against his palm. "Maybe we can take a minute."

He pressed kisses up my throat, steering me toward the dresser while I gathered my dress up over my hips.

"A moment." He lifted me onto the dresser, his mouth finding mine. The soft sound of his zipper followed, then his fingers grazed my pussy as he pushed aside my panties.

My breath came in shallow pants, eager, wanton, then stuck in my throat as he entered me.

"Ahhh." I gripped his ass as he fucked me hard and fast, rocking the dresser as our cries rose in a crescendo toward release.

This. I needed this. Him.

We were going to be late to the ball, and I didn't give a shit.

By the time we got to the ball, the event was well underway. Music, dancing, revelry. This was a celebration of freedom. Of a new beginning for humanity, and everyone was here. Gabriel and I slipped in, but going unnoticed with my wings wasn't realistic, and before we knew it, we were surrounded by people wanting to thank us for all our help.

Gabriel kept hold of my hand as I greeted people and

chatted with them. Faces were beginning to blur when a well-loved face filled my vision.

Jamie smiled down at me warmly. "I wanted to say thank you for everything. We're so grateful to you."

He didn't remember me, not from before the Purge, and not from when we'd met in the Golden City before he went into the mixer. All memory of me was gone. I was a stranger to him, a celestial. The woman tucked against his side who was looking up at him with adoration was his world now.

Better this way.

He was happy.

He was reborn.

That was all that mattered.

"You're welcome." I returned his smile. "Take care of each other."

"We will," the woman said. He kissed her on her head, and they slipped into the crowd.

"Does it hurt to see him?" Gabriel asked.

"Not anymore." I turned my face up to him. "My Jamie is gone. I'll never forget him. He taught me what love was, and I'm thankful for that."

"In that case," Gabriel said, "we should dance."

He swept me into his arms and onto the dance floor, and for a few hours, I was just a woman in love in the arms of the angel that loved her back.

MY SUMMONS HAD BEEN CLEAR, to report straight to Lucifer upon my return, and so Gabriel and I parted ways as soon as we got to heaven with a promise to find each other later.

My heels clipped on marble as I made my way to Lucifer's chambers. She'd built a replica of her Gehenna fortress in heaven down to the exact books on the shelves. It was her happy place, and one I knew she spent all her spare time in.

I found her curled up in an armchair with a large tome, a mug of some beverage on the table beside her.

"Don't you have work to do?" I fell into the seat opposite and kicked off my boots. The first month that I'd been working on New Hope City, I'd come back here often enough for this fortress replica to feel like home too, and Lucifer, well, it was impossible not to love her, despite her mercurial temper.

"I'm glad you're back," she said. "Shemyaza has been clomping about like a bear with a sore head the past few days. He wanted to join you for the ball, but I refused to let him."

"Why not?"

She arched a brow. "You reek of the aroma of new love and its consummation."

She didn't mean literally, of course, because celestials in heaven didn't need to wash and shower; we were cleansed always.

"You wanted me to have time with Gabriel."

"Not wanted, needed."

"What do you mean?"

She held up a finger and canted her head, and then a slight smirk curled her lips. "Shemyaza has been alerted to your arrival. Go to him. I will speak with you all tomorrow."

My curiosity warred with my need to see Shem.

Lucifer leaned forward and took my hand. "Take the pleasures and the freedom to enjoy them while you can, little sister." She turned back to her book, dismissing me, and I knew better than to push her to clarify.

She'd satisfy my curiosity when she was good and ready and not before.

I slipped my boots back on and went in search of Shem.

HEAVEN WAS A VAST PLACE, filled with light and peace and training arenas where the celestials could beat the shit out of each other because, yes, we had a lot of pent-up energy, and combat was a great way to siphon it off. God had created celestials to be his warriors, after all. To protect his creations and combat any beings that threatened that.

I found Shem in the arena beating the shit out of a celestial I didn't know, his fist making contact with the celestial's face over and over, but he faltered as I stepped onto the viewing balcony, then stopped altogether.

The celestial backed up, hands raised. "Shemyaza, I'm done."

Shem fixed his stunning neon blue eye on me, and my mouth went dry. He was formidable with his golden skin, and his sun-streaked hair, and those shoulders, perfect to hold on to, to dig my nails into when riding him.

His nostrils flared, and he jerked his head toward the exit before striding off.

That was my cue.

I knew what he needed, and I was ready to give it to him.

I caught up to him in the corridor beyond, and he slipped his hand into mine. We picked up the pace, our goal privacy.

Thank fuck his quarters weren't far.

We fell into his room, and he kicked the door shut before lifting me off my feet and shoving me against it.

There was no need for words as we willed our clothes away so our bodies could kiss.

I wrapped my legs around his waist and bit back a moan as he filled me then fucked me against the door, hard, fast, hungry, until my head filled with light and his name spilled from my lips like a mantra.

Release came and built again as he refused to let me go, staying deep inside me as we slipped to the floor, mouths melded, bodies moving in a rhythm that felt inevitable.

"Missed you," he groaned into my mouth.

"Missed you too."

He gripped my throat. "Even with Gabriel inside you?"

My eyes fluttered closed as he applied pressure. "No. Not then. Then it was only him."

He nipped at my bottom lip. "Now it will be only me. Because right now, this is mine."

There was no restraint as he pounded me, tearing strangled cries of twisted pleasure from my lips as hot tears leaked from my eyes until release washed over me, painful in its intensity—a flavor that only Shem could provide.

His hand slipped from my throat to my collarbones, and he hovered over me, his dark eyes devouring me. "I fucking missed you."

I smiled up at him. "Then show me how much. Again."

LUCIFER'S SUMMONS came at dawn, tearing me from Shem's arms and taking us both to the antechamber to Lucifer's audience chamber.

Bastian and Gabriel were already there, and they were surprised to see us.

"Summons?" Gabriel asked.

"Yes," Shem said.

Another figure filled the arch behind us, and it was my turn to blink in surprise. "Kabiel."

He inclined his head, his pale eyes wary. "I was summoned."

"Yes, so were we," Gabriel said.

"What do you think she wants?" Bastian said.

"I have no idea." But the fact she'd summoned us all meant it involved us all—which could be good, or it could be bad. What if she made me stop seeing them? What if she asked me to choose?

No. No, I wouldn't do that. I couldn't. If I couldn't have them all, then I wouldn't have any of them.

The doors to Lucifer's audience chamber finally swung open, and I led the way inside. She stood alone, dressed in dark slacks and a blue shirt, surrounded by a sea of gray and white—floors, drapes, walls. It made my eyes hurt.

The doors closed behind our party, and she fixed her dark gaze on us. "I've called you here today because I have a task for you all. One which I am now certain that you are equipped to take on." She smiled, but it didn't quite meet her eyes. "This world is not the only one which was abandoned by God. This heaven is not his first haven, and we are not his only celestials. I would not be surprised if there was another Lucifer out there somewhere. God has a compulsion to create, but not necessarily to maintain, and I believe that is why he made me his heir." Her mouth tightened. "To fix the worlds he allowed to fall into disrepair, and there are many." She shook her head. "Worlds on the brink of collapse. Worlds crying out for aid. I can hear them now. Their pleas, their pain. I cannot ignore them, but I will not abandon my post here either. So I need you to go in my place, little sister."

She wanted me to leave? "You're sending me away?"

Her stance softened. "I wish I did not have to, but you are the only one I can trust with the monumental task of helping these other worlds."

"I don't understand. How can I help?"

"With the power I will bestow upon you and your team." She looked at the guys. "The celestials who will support you. Guide you and love you."

My gaze shot to Kabiel, and his eyes flared.

"Kabiel and I are not...We're not."

"There is time," Lucifer said. "There is hope. There is power in the connection between you all. You must maintain it. You must work together. This is my task for you."

She wanted us to leave heaven. To go to another world and help it from being destroyed. Panic filled me.

"I don't know if I can do this. I can't even get my wings to hide."

She smiled gently. "But you will learn. You will grow, and when the time comes for you to take my place, you will be ready."

Her words were filled with conviction enough for the both of us.

"Are you all ready for the next chapter in your existences?"

The guys gathered close around me, lending me their support and assent.

It was time to turn the page. "We're ready."

LUCIFER

There are truths, there are lies, and then there are the stories we tell ourselves. The tales we weave in the dead of night to consolidate the past and pave the way for a desirable future.

"Mama? Are you listening?" Adiana says, looking up from her painting. "Do you like pink flowers or yellow flowers?"

"I like them both." I stroke her fiery tresses, hair typical of her kind. "But I like blue flowers the best. The same sapphire shade as your eyes."

She smiles up at me with adoration. "Me too, Mama."

She mixes paints together to get the correct shade of blue. She's so small, but she will grow in power. Her kind mature slowly; at least another decade will pass until she is an adult, maybe more—after all, she is a new breed. An abomination.

But I've claimed her as mine.

"Mama, tell me a story."

"Once upon a time, there was a powerful woman whose father locked her away in a nightmare."

"Why?"

"Because he was afraid of her power and what she would become." I curb a sneer. "Some prophecy, some terrible thing on the horizon...and so he took part of her power from her before she was strong enough to protect it, and he locked her away."

"What did she do?"

"She waited, and she grew stronger, and then she discovered an amazing thing: she could walk the dream realm. Her body was trapped, but her mind was not, and with that power, she reached out of her prison to whisper into the minds of those that might help her. Powerful beings whose greed and ambition would eventually set her free."

"And did she? Did she go free?"

The Dominion did their part in fracturing the relic to weaken the fabric of Gehenna, and Shemyaza, he never knew how I drove his actions, his conviction that the relic pieces must be found. And even Father's backup plan to keep me contained ended up working in my favor. They ended themselves when they should have ended me... together. That was the story Father wrote.

But I plan to write a different one.

"Mama?" Adiana tugs on my sleeve. "Did she escape?"

My lips curve in a smile. "With cunning, and wiles, and a story of her own. Yes, she did. Yes, she did."

If you loved Rue's story, then make sure to check out Stalk the Dark coming May 2024.

And if you haven't read The Demons of Morningstar or Wolves of Hawthorne Cove, you're missing out. Heck, just check out my backlist.

OTHER BOOKS BY DEBBIE CASSIDY

You can find a list of Debbie's books on her website debbiecassidyauthor.com or on her Amazon Author Page.

There are so many worlds to choose from.

Happy reading.

ABOUT THE AUTHOR

Debbie Cassidy lives in England, Bedfordshire, with her three kids and very supportive husband. Coffee and chocolate biscuits are her writing fuels of choice, and she is still working on getting that perfect tower of solitude built in her back garden. Obsessed with building new worlds and reading about them, she spends her spare time daydreaming and conversing with the characters in her head—in a totally non-psychotic way, of course. She writes Urban Fantasy Romance, Paranormal Reverse Harem Romance, and Sci Fi Romance.

Stay in touch with Debbie Cassidy.

Join her Newsletter

Hang out in her Facebook Reader Group

or

Follow her on Bookbub

Printed in Great Britain
by Amazon

39301976R00152